AMBER UNDERCOVER

D0242584

LONDON BOROUGH OF
RICHMOND UPON THAMES

DISCARDED

90710 000 467 713

Askews & Holts	31-Mar-2021

RICHMOND UPON THAMES

RTWH

LIBRARY SERVICE

wh...
me ...

OXFORD
UNIVERSITY PRESS

Great Clarendon Street, Oxford OX2 6DP
Oxford University Press is a department of the University of Oxford.
It furthers the University's objective of excellence in research, scholarship,
and education by publishing worldwide. Oxford is a registered trade mark
of Oxford University Press in the UK and in certain other countries

Copyright © Em Norry 2021

The moral rights of the author have been asserted

Database right Oxford University Press (maker)

First published 2021

All rights reserved. No part of this publication may be reproduced,
stored in a retrieval system, or transmitted, in any form or by any means,
without the prior permission in writing of Oxford University Press,
or as expressly permitted by law, or under terms agreed with the appropriate
reprographics rights organization. Enquiries concerning reproduction
outside the scope of the above should be sent to the Rights Department,
Oxford University Press, at the address above

You must not circulate this book in any other binding or cover
and you must impose this same condition on any acquirer

British Library Cataloguing in Publication Data

Data available

ISBN: 978-0-19-277473-6

1 3 5 7 9 10 8 6 4 2

Printed in Great Britain

Paper used in the production of this book is a natural,
recyclable product made from wood grown in
sustainable forests.The manufacturing process
conforms to the environmental regulations
of the country of origin.

EM NORRY

AMBER UNDER COVER

OXFORD
UNIVERSITY PRESS

Weeds are flowers too,
once you get to know them.

A.A. Milne

CHAPTER 1

'Press B,' I instructed Vi, hovering behind her in the lift as the squeaky doors eased closed. 'B for basement.'

'Sure?' Her voice shook as her finger paused over the button.

'Absolutely,' I said.

In this deserted army base the basement was the only place we hadn't explored.

Our teammates Connor and Milly turned to each other. He nodded reluctantly. Clearly, he wished he'd come up with the idea himself. The second Vi and I met him, it was obvious he enjoyed being in charge and didn't like taking orders.

We'd found the hidden lift, which, along with the basement, hadn't been marked on the map for some reason. I figured the basement must be a secret underground bunker. It *had* to be where the nuclear warheads were. We had to be on the right track.

If we didn't shut them down . . . I didn't want to think about what would happen. This mission couldn't go wrong. We'd been at it for what felt like hours. I was tired and thirsty and could have killed for a can of lemonade—but adrenaline pumped through me, keeping me alert.

Focus, Amber. Focus. OK. I had this. I could only do my best, right? Right.

Would this lead to success, or was this a trap? I prayed that the code sequence we'd found earlier would get us into the bunker. It *had* to work, or in a few hours half of Europe would be obliterated.

'When the lift stops, look for concealed entrances to the bunker,' Connor declared.

'OK, chief.' I smiled at Vi, who grinned back. 'You got it!' I wasn't planning on obeying Connor and we both knew it.

As we descended the five levels underground, Vi's eyes widened nervously so I flashed her my reassuring *this-will-be-fine* best friend smile, even though my brain squawked the opposite. We'd spent ages following dead leads upstairs—we could be too late. My stomach felt crammed full of butterflies flapping their wings in overdrive.

Finally, the lift settled with a clunk. Vi instinctively reached for my hand and I squeezed hers.

The doors had opened onto a wide, empty tunnel. A drab sight: rough, exposed grey stone walls and fluorescent strip lights running along the ceiling. Along the top of the walls were thick, cracked plastic pipes. Rank and very gloomy.

'What does *that* mean?' Vi asked, nudging me as we stepped out, her eyes flicking up to a section of striped yellow and black tape marked 'caution' lining the tunnel's archway, flapping loose. 'Isn't that usually a warning?' Her voice was shaking. Though part of me wanted to immediately evacuate the building, it was my job to keep Vi calm, which weirdly enough always calmed me down too. A win-win.

'It's alright, Vi. Don't worry.' I told her.

It was noisy this deep underground. Were we close to an engine room? It sounded as if there was rushing water nearby. The strip lights flickered. I didn't know if they were faulty, or if, by activating the secret lift, we'd tripped a motion sensor.

Better not be a bad sign.

Vi squinted. 'Now what?'

'We need to get into the bunker,' I replied, looking around.

'Exactly what I thought!' said Connor, and to my

surprise he and Milly dropped behind us. Vi and I spent the next twenty seconds trying not to smirk at each other, which turned out to be a pretty effective anti-anxiety technique.

Although the tunnel was long, our destination was clear: a huge metal door at the far end. It looked like the only place to try. Everything we'd done so far had brought us in this direction. I had no intention of failing now. Not after all the effort we'd made. But *something* wasn't right. I just couldn't put my finger on what.

'Five minutes to lockdown,' an automated voice tonelessly announced. I flinched. Despite telling myself to stay calm, my heart was hammering. I wiped my clammy hands down my trousers.

'Is that lockdown *before* the missiles go off and we're all dead, or lockdown meaning we'll be locked in?' Vi wailed.

I had no idea and wasn't intending on hanging around to find out. We had to succeed in our mission—we had no other choice.

'Stay cool, Vi!' I said, loud and firm, making myself heard over the clanging pipes. 'We're nearly there. We can do this!'

We sprinted towards the bunker door about a hundred metres in front of us. Vi tore past me, of course; her sprinting skills are amazing. I followed, my trainers slapping against the concrete. I heard Connor and Milly behind me, panting for breath.

I caught up with Vi and we leaned, gasping, against the smooth metal door.

'Look, this keypad *has* to open the bunker,' Vi said, pointing to a metal numbered grid next to the door. 'And we already have the code!'

I scanned the keypad. That seemed too simple, or maybe we were *supposed* to think it was too simple.

I reached out, my fingers over the keypad.

'Want me to try it?'

'Yes!' the others said, coming up behind me.

'What's the code again?' Vi asked, looking calmer now.

'Two yellow, seven green, and four blue,' Milly recited.

I quickly entered the code. *BLEEP!* And . . . nothing. I peered at the flashing keypad, resisting the urge to slam my hand against the bunker door in frustration.

'So . . . what now?' Connor asked, his eyebrows raised.

'Wait.' I shook my head. 'Let me think.'

He frowned. 'There isn't time to think!' he yelled. '*Move.* I'll handle this.' He shoved me to one side, not noticing Vi's grimace, and hammered at the keypad.

I craned my head to see what Connor's fingers were doing. Too late, he'd already entered some random sequence. His face fell when the lights blinked red. The monotone voice announced: 'Four minutes till lockdown.'

As Connor stepped back, Milly elbowed him, and they proceeded to flip through the brief we'd been given—checking we hadn't overlooked anything, I guess.

No time for cramming now, I thought, my brain spinning faster than Mum's tumble dryer. *What if the keypad is rigged? What if we don't get out? Maybe we took a wrong turn and were supposed to go in a different direction. Could there be another entrance? Did we miss a clue?*

Vi manoeuvred herself in front of the keypad. 'Here, I'll try!' she said, punching the first number in again.

The bleeping keypad indicated another unsuccessful attempt. Three tries now. How many strikes did we have left?

'Less than four minutes!' Vi yelped. 'Maybe we should go back upstairs. That desk behind the door? Did you check the drawers? I can't remember . . . I can't remember if I opened the last one!'

'Violet. Stop. Panicking,' I said, through gritted

teeth. My friend was smart, but easily flustered. She'd been like this since we were little. Impulsive, leaping into things without thinking them through. I preferred to stand back and consider all the options before taking any action. Maybe it was an only child thing.

I needed to block Vi out for a while, if we were ever going to get out of here.

Focus.

There was a small hole in the door. I squatted and put my eye against it but couldn't see anything. *Isn't that where a door handle would usually be?*

Putting my palms against the cool metal, I peered closely at the door itself. Could a handle have been removed? What if a handle was needed to open it? The code might be correct after all.

Think, Amber. Think! What was I seeing, or *not* seeing? We'd tried the colour and number combos. Fail.

I cleared my throat. 'Right.'

Sometimes . . . going backwards is the only way to move forward.

'We're never going to get out!' Milly wailed, and I could practically see the sweat on her forehead.

'We've messed it all up!' cried Vi.

'People, arguing is pointless!' I said, raising my voice. *Oops!* That *was* loud. Even Vi looked surprised.

'I mean . . . We need to work together, and fast,' I said more calmly. 'Connor, try variations of the code we know, and be methodical about—'

'*Methodeee*-what?'

'Enter *one* digit at a time, starting with the number one and go through in order, up to nine. Vi and Milly, could you search the tunnel? I think someone might have removed the door handle. Maybe it's hidden somewhere? Unless it's fallen through the other side, but if so . . . then . . . we're stuffed. I'll retrace our steps, alright?'

I sprinted to the lift and turned to see Vi halfway behind me, feeling the pipes along the walls, while Milly searched around the door on her hands and knees.

'Three minutes to lockdown.'

I ran into the lift as soon as the doors opened. Glanced up. No loose roof panels to conceal anything. I jabbed the buttons. Couldn't believe I was heading up again, wasting precious time. What had we missed?

The neon sign above the door flickered *ALERT*— strobe-like, in red letters. In the doorway, I stared at cracked paintings on the walls outside the lift. Ransacked filing cabinets stood with open drawers. I looked back at the neon sign. Red. Red meant . . .

danger.

Think, Amber!

It had to be something obvious. Something staring me in the face. I backed into the corridor and stared up at the sign again.

Was that a flash of something? I dragged over a chair and stood on it. Yes, something was glinting below the sign. I reached up and felt along the wall until my fingers touched something smooth. Under the flashing sign, and easy to miss, was a length of metal.

Yes! I snatched the door handle.

'Two minutes till lockdown!'

I couldn't stab the lift buttons fast enough. The second the doors opened, I screeched, 'Hey!' but my throat was so dry, my voice barely squeaked.

'HEY!' I shouted again, surprising myself with the volume. I didn't usually shout. 'I've found the handle!'

I sprinted along the corridor. Halfway down, I grabbed Vi, pulling at her sleeve and we ran and ran, breathing hard, arms pumping, towards the bunker door.

'Did you hear me?!' I screeched to the others. The corridor seemed to stretch for miles.

Milly stood next to the keypad, but Connor was

blocking my view of the door.

'Connor!' I threw the handle to him. He dived forward, catching it.

Milly bashed the code into the keypad and at the same time Connor slotted the handle into the hole. The robotic voice started repeating: 'Lockdown! Lockdown in three, two . . .'

Connor leaned on the handle, pressing his weight against it, and the door flew open. Milly and Connor dashed through.

It worked!

My ears were full of the beeping alarm.

Vi and I hurtled through the door too, just as the lights in the corridor snapped off and everything went black.

CHAPTER 2

After the darkness of the corridor, the light that hit us was blindingly white. I squinted, holding one hand over my eyes.

'Amber, we did it.' Vi let out a deep breath and squeezed my arm. '*We made it.*'

'You mean we *won't* be blown to smithereens today?' I joked, catching my breath. We'd entered a large white room. 'Escape Zone' posters plastered the walls.

As Connor and Milly high-fived each other by the door, I noticed a woman in the corner, standing next to a couple of purple armchairs. She finished speaking into a walkie-talkie and flapped a clipboard at us.

'Nice work, Team C,' she said.

Vi and I exchanged a smile. Inside, I was

air-punching because I'd loved it—the entire experience—even the prickle of sweat when things got stressful. Knowing that it was down to us—me!—to save the day was terrifying, but it had focused my mind like nothing else. The only similar feeling was maybe on the running track, when I concentrated on pacing myself during my long-distance trials. It was the same mindset, working out the best way to reach the end point.

My first escape room experience had been an intense adrenaline rush. Not surprising that escape rooms were so popular—what a natural high.

'This place was the biggest and best I've seen.' Connor slapped me on the back. 'I would have worked out the handle was missing, eventually. But you were so quick!'

'Yeah, teamwork makes the dream work,' Milly sneered, hanging off him like a scarf.

The woman with the clipboard raised an eyebrow at them, then gave me a long, lingering look. She cleared her throat. 'This is the chill-out zone where we started,' she said. 'Your lockers are over there. But if you go through that archway, you'll find drinks and snacks laid out. Take a few minutes to relax before you head out into the real world.'

She nodded at us, giving me another intense

look—had I done something wrong?—and then twiddled buttons on her walkie-talkie before clipping it to her belt. I was still in *Take Note Of Everything Because You Never Know Its Importance* mode.

Along one wall were the lockers we'd dumped our stuff into and above them was the exit sign.

'How cool was that?' I said to Vi. 'I could do it all again right now.'

'Yeah, it was fun.' But Vi's smile had faded. Was she annoyed because I'd saved the day? Guess she hadn't been the centre of attention like she usually was.

'Did it freak you out?' I asked.

Vi shrugged. 'It was cool, but it seemed . . . too real. A bit intense. And I wish I'd been more chilled, especially in front of Mr Know-it-all.'

'Maybe next time,' I said, grinning.

As we walked through to get our refreshments, I was still thinking about how critical Vi had been. Lately, I kept worrying that I was annoying her. Not on purpose, but just because we were into different things. She wanted to try the after-school drama club, but that was my idea of absolute hell. No way would I join that, even if it was with my best mate. Dressing up and pretending to be someone else? I hated being the centre of attention.

I'd told Vi to go ahead and join the drama club anyway, but she didn't want to sign up without me. For someone quite confident, she got really uncomfortable about trying new things on her own. That's how I'd been roped into this Escape Zone experience, although to be fair, it seemed I'd enjoyed it way more than she had.

On a glass table in front of us was an ice bucket filled with cans of fizzy drink. My dream. I grabbed a lemonade, wiped the condensation away on my trousers and cracked it open, glugging half immediately. Vi *ummed* and *ahhed* before choosing a mocha-frappe-cino-something. *Ewww*. Cold coffee was her latest obsession. I thought coffee tasted like dirt, but I'd never turn down a hot chocolate with whipped cream, chocolate sprinkles, and marshmallows.

Vi took a pineapple cube from a tall jar of sweets then turned to me.

'You really kept your cool in there, Ambs,' she said. 'It was pretty impressive.'

'*Oh*. It takes me saving you from an imminent nuclear blast to appreciate my true worth, does it, Violet McFadden? Are you suggesting the past ten years of our friendship have been meaningless?' I wiggled my eyebrows at her.

Vi laughed. 'And you claim you can't act,' she said, affectionately, passing me a lemon sherbet. 'You totally channelled a superhero in there.'

Oh no, please don't hassle me about the drama group again . . .

'Seriously, I mean it. Like . . . you morphed into a leader, right in front of my eyes. *Very* cool. Now, how about revealing more of *that* Amber at school, hmm?'

She crunched down hard on her sweet.

'Right.' My cheeks heated up. Vi had a point, it was like my alter ego had come out or something. The last few months, I'd had a really hard time. Over the holidays, I'd had this massive growth spurt and people kept commenting on it, saying, 'How's the weather up there?' and other stupid things. I'd grown four inches in six months. Even though Mum and Dad are tall, I'm self-conscious about towering over my classmates. If I'm honest, it's pushed me into my shell more than usual.

The thing is, I don't know what had happened in the Escape Zone, but somehow, with everyone squabbling and urgent decisions needing to be made, a feeling of calm had swept over me. Everything had gone into slow motion. Working out the puzzles had been relaxing, and it had been a total buzz having to remember what we'd noticed before in the other rooms, seeing if anything came into play later.

I looked over at Milly and Connor throwing peanuts into each other's mouths. Before today I couldn't have imagined telling two strangers what to do, but back there it hadn't bothered me; if anything, it had given me a thrill.

The clipboard woman dipped her head through the archway. 'Before you leave, I need to talk to you.'

Vi and I straightened up into our school assembly positions.

'Well, just to remind you that revealing details about today isn't permitted. You recall signing the non-disclosure agreements?'

As if to emphasize this point, two security cameras attached to light fittings swivelled our way, little red sensors blinking.

Vi grinned nervously. 'Afraid we'll leak your secrets?'

The woman gave a patient smile. 'Hopefully, your *free* experience via the HappySnap ad you answered, in exchange for assisting us, was fun. But the experience is still being developed. We'd hate for our . . . competitors to hear how we run things. Keeping spoilers to yourselves is appreciated.'

She pressed a wall panel and a concealed cupboard swung open. She handed us each a red paper bag with EZ written on the side. 'To say thank you.'

'Goody bags!' Vi tipped hers out onto the table and scanned the contents: money-off vouchers for local shops and a 2-4-1 cinema voucher, sweets, a keyring shaped like a cube, and a pen.

'Don't forget to collect your things.' Smiling mysteriously, the woman walked through the archway.

At the metal lockers, I stopped and smiled. 'Vi, look,' I said. 'The numbers of our lockers are the same!'

Vi wrinkled her nose. 'As what?'

'As the final code that opened the bunker door!'

'We get it, Sherlock,' Connor butted in, rolling his eyes. He slung his arm around Milly's shoulder, and they walked towards the exit.

I grabbed my jacket and bag. *Time to let it go.* The real world was definitely back.

Once the door banged behind them, Vi muttered: 'Was it my imagination, or were those two really annoying?'

'Totally annoying,' I admitted.

'Promise me that when I get a boyfriend, I won't be that useless.'

Boyfriend? She'd been talking about boys loads recently. I wasn't too bothered—but, along with her becoming friendlier with Terrible Two-Faced

Taylor, being less interested in schoolwork, and her drama obsession, it was yet another thing changing between us.

'Got anyone specific in mind?' I nudged her.

'Oh, you know . . . tall, dark, and handsome will suit me.' She tied her jumper around her waist, banging her locker door shut. 'Dinner round mine? Mum's dishing up baked beans because baby Sid is addicted, but they won't be the only thing.'

Aged four, during a soft-play lunch, agreeing that baked beans were a fate worse than death was what Vi and I had first bonded over. We'd both upended our bowls at the same time, baked beans oozing everywhere. We'd been best friends ever since. But I couldn't shake the feeling that maybe this forever friendship wasn't as set in stone as it always had been.

'Thanks Vi, but I'd best head straight home. Mum said she and Dad have something to discuss with me.'

'Ooh!' Vi made a face, and air quotes with her fingers. 'A "discussion"? What's that about, d'you think?'

'I've no idea.'

'They do know you've started your periods, right?'

'*Vi!*' I said, blushing. Nothing seemed to embarrass Vi.

'In that case it'll be the Being Safe Online talk or—' Her eyes widened, and she hissed. 'Oh, no, maybe that horrible statue your dad brought back from Egypt is actually some haunted artefact and your entire family is now cursed.'

Laughing, I put my hand over my mouth. 'Vi!' Sometimes she was so dramatic. 'I don't know. There have been . . . a lot of closed doors and whispers lately, so . . .' I shrugged.

'It can't be too bad. If it was divorce, you'd know.' Her sunny expression darkened for a moment. '*I* did.'

Vi's parents had got divorced a month after we'd started secondary school. It had messed her up for a while. She'd been moved out of the top sets and had really struggled. For a few months, she'd practically moved in with us. It was only in the last year that she'd been OK with it.

Vi fished her phone out of her bag and scrolled through her messages. 'Oh God, I can't wait to tell Layla about us crawling under that army netting when I virtually ripped my trousers . . .'

I nudged her. 'We're not supposed to tell anyone anything, remember?'

Vi rolled her eyes. '*Puh-leaze* . . .'

'Anyway, I thought you and Layla weren't friendly now? Not since she and Taylor got detention for trolling—'

'Tay and Lay!'

'They sound like a brand of crisps, don't they?'

'Layla's alright, actually. She helps me in maths.' Vi started texting, but something she'd said was playing on my mind. *Divorce?*

Things at home had been weird, lately. I'd only told Vi the half of it. She thought my family were so perfect and I always felt odd complaining, considering what she'd been through. The last few months had seen lots of closed doors: tears, raised voices about money, TV channels switched over, internet histories cleared. Were my parents planning to move? Had they lost their jobs? Were we in debt? Were my grandparents ill? Something major was going on, but I couldn't think what it might be.

Not divorce though. Please, not divorce.

CHAPTER 3

The second my key was in the door, Mum's voice rang out.

'Did you get them?'

'What?'

'Oh, Amber, it's you?'

'Who else would it be?' I called back, easing my shoes off. I hung up my coat and dumped my bag on the bottom step. Delicious smells came from the kitchen. *Mmm*. Spaghetti bolognese: my favourite.

But . . . Mum had a weekly dinner rota she worked through and today was only Wednesday. Spag bol was firmly reserved for Fridays. She made a huge batch for the freezer once a month; sometimes I helped. Last month she'd ditched her usual mammoth cooking session though. Yet another sign that something was on her mind.

So, either we had something to celebrate, or it was bad news and the spag bol was to soften the blow.

Which was it?

I went into the kitchen. Mum was pulling on oven gloves. She took out a tray of steaming cheesy garlic bread and slammed the oven door with her foot.

'Your dad's nipped out to get some bits for me.' Mum turned around and put the tray down on the worktop. 'How's Vi?'

'She's good. It's Tom's birthday soon, so their house is a bit crazed.'

The front door banged shut. 'They only had silverskin!' Dad bellowed, rushing into the kitchen and dumping a carrier bag onto the counter. 'And I couldn't remember if you liked those, but I got them anyway, because if you wake me up at 3 a.m. again . . .'

He turned and noticed me. 'Amber . . . er . . . how's your day been, pet?' He leaned over, kissing my cheek.

'Why are we having spag bol?' I asked, taking knives and forks out of the cutlery drawer and setting the table.

Dad's eyes flicked to Mum dishing up. She passed him a bowl of green salad leaves.

I looked between them, trying to decode their body language which I was normally good at because Dad was the most transparent person ever.

'OMG, we're getting a dog?!' I jiggled my legs excitedly.

I'd wanted a pet for years. I liked cats but Mum was allergic. Vi had an adorable cockapoo called Monty that her mum got after the divorce, and although I walked him sometimes, it wasn't the same as having your own. I'd begged for my own puppy for ages.

Dad glanced at Mum, shaking his head before sitting down. 'Nope. Sorry, love. No dogs.'

Oh. My shoulders slumped as I heaped salad leaves onto my plate.

'Amber.' Mum rubbed my shoulder before easing herself awkwardly into a chair, as if she had backache. 'It just wouldn't be practical, especially . . . now.'

Mum and Dad gave each other the secret Parent Eye Signal meaning: *'Ready?'*

I nibbled round the edges of a slice of garlic bread dripping with melted cheese.

'We'll have a new addition to the family soon enough,' Dad said, looking dreamy-eyed.

'My due date, oddly enough, is on Halloween.'

Mum reached across the table and took hold of Dad's hand.

YOU WHAT?

'Halloween?' I spluttered, spraying cheese across the table. Due date? It couldn't be. Nope, my brain had heard 1 + 2 and come up with 12.

'We wanted to wait—'

'Until we were sure everything was OK.'

Their voices sounded distorted, overlapping like some freaky meme.

'Whoa, *hold on*!' I cried loudly. 'Can you explain what's going on, as if I'm a child, which I am, by the way, in case you'd forgotten.'

'Love,' Mum said softly. 'I'm pregnant.'

'But, you're *old*!' I wailed, unable to stop myself from being so mean.

Dad stifled a laugh. 'Sweetheart, Mum's not old.'

She pushed her fringe out of her eyes. 'I *am* forty-three,' she said. 'Amber has a point. I'm no spring chicken.'

'You're way too old to have a baby!' I stared at my plate, the spag bol looking blurry . . . because my eyes were full of tears. I dashed them away.

A stinking, noisy, dribbling baby crawling all over my stuff? I'd be doing exams soon too. *Nightmare! Nappies and noise. No sleep.*

'We know this is a shock,' Dad said. 'It was for us too.'

'I'll say!' Mum laughed. 'But, with three months to get used to the idea, we've finally come around. And we hope you will too, love. It's going to be quite the adventure!'

'Really?' I snapped. 'When I begged for a brother or sister, you went on about how special being an only child was! How you had more time and money and energy *just* for me. Was that just lies then?'

They looked at each other, shocked. Clearly, this wasn't how they thought I'd react.

I bolted out of the kitchen and grabbed my bag, then ran upstairs and slammed my bedroom door. On my bed, I rummaged in my bag for my phone and skimmed three messages from Vi.

I started to text: *Guess what bombshell my parents just exploded?* But, mid-text, I stopped, thumbs poised. Had to keep swallowing my tears.

Pregnant? Vi would squeal in delight. Now that Vi and her three brothers had got used to the divorce, her house was a chaotic, fun-filled mess. Her mum was relaxed and forgetful and there was never any privacy . . .

I loved being over at Vi's, but after a few hours it was like drowning—no space, ever. I was always pleased to get home. To the calm, order, and quiet.

Until now.

My shoulders slumped and I put my phone to one side. *Mum was pregnant!* I needed to think about this. I thought back to biology lessons. For a pregnancy to be 'viable', it took twelve weeks. Things could go wrong before that, which is why Mum and Dad had kept it secret for three whole months. All that whispering and all those hurriedly closed Google searches made sense now.

'Sweetheart?' Knuckles rapped softly against my door. 'Can I come in?'

I opened the door to see Mum leaning against the doorframe, looking concerned. I was still angry, but the sight of her worried face brought tears to my eyes.

'Oh, love,' she said, reaching out to hug me. I sort of dodged her hug and found my face reluctantly snuffled into her armpit instead. 'Are you freaking out?'

I nodded, my voice muffled. 'Maybe. I knew something was going on, but I wasn't expecting *this*. You know I like to . . . be prepared.'

'It's not what *I* was expecting either, honestly. Dad and I were together for ten years before we decided we wanted children. And it wasn't easy.' Her eyes misted over as she stared at my bed, still piled high with cuddly animals. 'Sometimes, it's difficult to become pregnant; you were the most wonderful surprise.'

I untangled myself and went over to sit on my bed. 'But I thought you wanted to go back to college?' I opened my laptop and switched it on.

'I did. I still do, when we've got more money. But what you said downstairs is partly correct. I'm *not* getting younger. Forty-three isn't old, but the opportunity to have more children won't be around for long. College isn't going anywhere. Things will change around here, but that doesn't have to be a bad thing! It's more responsibility for all of us. You're going to have someone who, in a few years' time, will look up to you. They'll think the world of you, Amber!' She smiled as though this was something I'd want to hear, but it was way too soon. I knew she was trying to 'involve' me, but I didn't *want* to be involved. I didn't want to be anyone's 'big sister', thanks.

Then I noticed the shadows under her eyes. Remembered how exhausted and emotional she'd been. There was no point getting into this now. Instead of saying what I really felt, I just nodded, and pulled my laptop closer to me.

'It's fine, Mum,' I told her. 'Honestly. But I really better get on with this homework.'

School was a twenty-minute walk from my house. Vi lived a few roads away and always knocked for me, so we walked in together. This time was usually when we chatted non-stop (we hardly had any lessons together, except P.E., and often did different things after school), but I couldn't stop thinking about the Baby. I didn't *want* things to change. I liked things as they were!

For some reason I hadn't worked out, I didn't want to tell Vi just yet. Even though we never kept secrets from each other, I needed to take it in myself first, before I confided in her. Besides, she'd never stop hassling me about why I wasn't happier, and I felt bad enough already.

'Are you up for this track race next month then?' Vi asked.

'Mmm,' I mumbled absently.

She took a huge bite out of a banana; she always ate on the move. 'Get out of the wrong side of bed this morning?'

This was a running joke between us because my bed was against a wall; there was literally only one side of the bed I could get out of. But I wasn't feeling the banter today.

'I dunno. Didn't sleep well,' I muttered. That was

true. I'd tossed and turned for ages, then dreamed about giant wailing baby twins smashing up my stuff.

'So . . . what was the big discussion then?' Vi asked, dumping the banana skin in the bin.

'Um . . . nothing, really.' I shrugged, hoping she'd drop it.

'Oh, go on. Yesterday it seemed like you were worried.'

Looking at her eager face, I felt terrible when I skirted round the truth.

'We're getting massive renovations done on the house. Big changes. I'm going to have to move rooms probably. Everything's going to be . . . completely and utterly different by Halloween.' That wasn't the half of it.

'Oh. *Huh.*' Vi's smile faltered. 'Weird what parents consider "news", right?'

'Right.'

Off the hook. *For now.*

'Sorry I didn't get around to replying to your messages. What was the one about Taylor's party?'

'Oh, yeah!' Vi said, excited. 'Layla's got me an invite!' Taking in my expression, she added, 'I mean, it's not like I *wanted* to go or anything, but it's cool to be invited?'

Taylor's parties were legendary for being extravagant (last year her dad hired a *troop* of dancers), and neither of us had ever been invited to one.

'Oh, right,' I said, trying to conceal my bewilderment. 'You're going to go then?' My phone vibrated in my coat pocket. I didn't receive loads of messages in the morning, unless it was Vi, or my parents. I brought my phone out and angled the screen away from Vi a little.

I've got a midwife appointment at 5. Want to come with me?

Yep. And there we had it—Baby taking priority, *already*. Oh God, Mum was going to want me there at every stage, wasn't she?

Can't. Got a thing after school, I texted back, feeling mean. But before I'd put my phone away it buzzed again.

No Mum . . . I really don't want to come with you! I thought.

But it wasn't from Mum.

Amber: based on your aptitude at EZ yesterday, we'd like you to trial our newest in-game VR format. Please respond YES or NO. Non-disclosure applies.

What? I stopped walking to read the text again. I peeked at Vi, expecting her phone to buzz any minute too.

'What is it?' Vi asked, craning her neck to see my screen.

'Check your phone.'

She pulled out her mobile and stared at it. 'Nothing. Why?'

'I just got a message from that Escape Zone place.' I held out my phone for her to read the message.

'Oh.' She tried to sound cheerful. 'That's . . . Wow, you've been invited back?'

'I guess.' My heart thumped as I said, casually, 'You've not got anything?'

She touched her screen a few times and grimaced.

'Maybe they got your number wrong?' I suggested, brightly.

'Maybe.' She shrugged and shoved her phone in her pocket. 'It doesn't matter.'

They wanted to see me again! I must have impressed them. Yesterday had been such a buzz. But I didn't want to do this without Vi . . . or did I?

'Look,' she said, tying her long blonde hair up into a high ponytail. 'Don't worry about me, it seemed more your thing anyway, didn't it? All that problem-solving. And yes, in answer to your question, damn right I'm going to Taylor's party if I'm lucky enough to have scored an invite! I'll report back.'

CHAPTER 4

At 4 p.m. I pressed Escape Zone's entrance buzzer again, wondering if it was broken because I'd been standing outside for ages.

As soon as I'd texted back **YES** this morning, I was sent a request to attend the trial—today, after school! That didn't leave me any time to really prepare, or go over what had worked so well yesterday, but maybe that's what they wanted. Anyway, I was glad to have something to do. This would beat going home and feigning interest in Mum's midwife appointment, or even worse being dragged along. I felt bad for Vi, though. She'd been pretty normal at lunch, but it was obvious she felt left out. I reckon that's why she opted to do extra sprint training after school.

The metal door clicked ajar. 'Hello?' I called out, nervously. As I pushed the door open and stepped inside, a figure smoothly glided towards me.

'Amber Roberts.' The same woman as the day before greeted me, but this time she was dressed head-to-toe in white.

'Am I early?' I said. 'I haven't seen anyone else.'

'There *is* no one else,' she said strangely. 'Only you.'

What?

She closed the door behind us and squinted at her tablet. 'I mean . . . for today.' She smiled: bleached teeth, perfectly straight. 'Today is a solo project. You'll be testing a VR prototype.'

'A what now?'

'Virtual reality.'

Gaming? Not really my thing.

'Um. I don't know much about virtual reality.'

'That's fine. We're looking for experienced and non-experienced users. We work on lots of different projects here; this is one of many. Follow me please.'

As we took a sharp right into a narrow corridor, I didn't recognize anything from yesterday. It seemed we were in an entirely different section of the enormous building. Where the corridor ended, the woman opened a door and ushered me into a room. The only thing in there was a giant see-through plastic ball, like the world's biggest hamster toy.

On a table next to that were goggles, a headset, and thick gloves.

The room had no windows, only white walls. I slipped a hand into my pocket, fingers tightening around my mobile. My nerves tingled. *Should I be worried?* At least Vi knew exactly where I was.

'Your progress will be monitored from the control room.'

Control room? Scenes from dystopian films rushed through my mind.

'What am I supposed to do?'

'Sign the non-disclosure agreement on the table and then please put on the headset, goggles, and gloves and step into the bubble. The equipment will enable you to pick things up and sense objects within the VR environment. When you're ready to start, press the TEST button. You'll receive instructions through the headset. Good luck.'

She smiled before closing the door.

Good luck? *Oh-kay*.

I put on the headset; the earpiece was tiny. The goggles were like skiing goggles and covered half my face. The plastic bubble reminded me of those balls I'd seen people roll down hills in. I stepped inside. This was going to be weird.

Stretching my arms out, I could touch the sides. I

slipped the gloves on and pressed the TEST button.

The goggles lit up like a private mini-cinema screen. Images of a woman with a black bob, wearing a red baseball cap, flashed up in front of me. Then another image, of a woman with tanned skin and grey cropped hair, replaced her.

The word MEMORIZE appeared and a digital clock counted down from ten, the images fading. Along the bottom of the screen scrolled the words:

You: Tourist.

Accessory: Camera.

Mission: Photograph targets meeting.

Warning: Targets are monitored. Do not identify yourself, or arouse suspicion, under any circumstances.

BEGIN!

I found myself in the centre of a bustling marketplace—somewhere like Morocco, judging by the vivid colours. The sky was bright blue with wisps of summer-day clouds. Market stalls lined cobbled streets, and baskets hung off the stalls, overflowing with fruit, silver jewellery, and silk scarves. Moving my hand back and forth, I pushed aside the dangling scarves blocking my view.

I looked ahead. Couldn't see either of my targets just yet. I inhaled. Tangy citrus filled the air. Hearing jangling, I turned to see a barefooted woman wearing an ankle bracelet with bells. And behind her, a few metres away, a woman in a red baseball cap: my target! I needed to follow her and take a photo. I looked down and glimpsed a camera around my neck.

Suddenly, people crowded in front of me and my target got swallowed up. How was I supposed to keep track of her now?

I moved forwards, scanning the crowd. Red was everywhere: flowers, clothes, ribbons, shopping bags . . . I hardly knew where to look. Flicking my eyes from side to side, on high alert for my target, I walked fast, sometimes lingering at market stalls, pretending I was browsing, trying to keep my tourist cover.

But time felt like it was passing quickly; I needed to speed things up. *Where was she?*

I came to the end of a row of market stalls and entered a crowded piazza. Every other step, I bumped into a table, or a waiter carrying drinks. Schoolchildren and ladies with tiny dogs on leads were everywhere I turned. My heart pounding furiously, I ducked and weaved, as if I was dancing— quite the workout!

I needed to stay calm; to stop and look. I took a deep breath and slowly scanned the surrounding square with its boutiques and cafés, holding my camera as if I was looking to capture the perfect tourist snap.

There she is!

Bobbed baseball-cap lady stood with her back to me, outside a shop with suitcases and handbags in the window.

I hung back, half-hidden by a parasol directly across from the shop and watched her walk inside.

Excellent. I couldn't possibly lose her now. I darted across the square and opened the door, but then . . . I froze. The shop was tiny! I hid behind the nearest pillar, and studied the leather purses on a table, cursing myself. I should have stayed closer and moved quicker.

A bell rang. The shop door opened again, and the other target walked in. I hadn't noticed her before, but maybe *this* was their meeting point?

She walked over to baseball-cap lady. *This was my moment!* I needed to photograph them together. I raised my camera to take a photo.

I jumped. Both targets were now glaring right at me.

Amber, you idiot.

I couldn't take a picture here—this wasn't what a tourist would photograph.

Quickly, I headed outside, my hands trembling as I gripped the camera. Hopefully I hadn't roused their suspicions. I couldn't go back in the shop, but maybe it wasn't too late? Maybe the targets would come out?

I waited forever, but finally, the shop door opened and the woman with grey cropped hair came out. *Yes!* I had her! I zoomed in with my camera, ready to take a shot, but no one else followed. Cropped-hair lady crossed the square and disappeared.

My visor shimmered and darkened. MISSION FAILED flickered in red capital letters.

Removing the earpiece, and taking the gloves and goggles off, I stepped out of the giant ball and blinked, trying to get used to white walls again after those incredible colours. I'd blown it! No more Escape Zone invites now.

My shoulders sagged. I realized how disappointed in my performance I was.

The door opened and the same woman who'd shown me in said, 'Come with me, please.'

Frustration and adrenaline spiralled through me as I followed her out. My heart was still beating too fast, and I kept babbling, 'I'm sorry. I don't really—'

'You can explain in a moment.'

Halfway along the corridor, she paused by a blank

wall before holding her palm up. I felt my breathing gradually calm down. A pair of wall panels slid open.

'In you go,' she said. 'She's expecting you.'

Who, what?

I stepped in. The wall glided closed behind me and I shivered—creepy!

An elegantly dressed (emerald pencil skirt, matching fingernails, red suede high heels) dark-haired woman sat on a cream leather sofa, sipping from a tiny china cup.

'Please, sit down, Amber.' Her voice was rich. She indicated a chair opposite her. Was she the CEO? Or the game creator? 'Earl Grey, or a macchiato, perhaps?'

I sat. 'I don't drink tea or coffee, but thanks.'

'Something soft, then? Water, orange juice, milk?' This woman was all business.

'Do you have any lemonade?'

'I should have remembered you like a little . . . *fizz,*' she said, smiling and putting down her cup. When she smiled, her face transformed, and instead of looking like a scary headmistress, she looked more like an old-time film star. Her glossy black hair curled around her perfectly made-up face in soft waves. The only time I'd ever seen anyone this polished was when Mum went to parents' evening at school. I hadn't expected the gaming world to be so . . . glamorous.

'I don't get it—why should you have remembered what I like?' I frowned, confused, trying not to stare at her too hard.

'I'll explain presently.' She glanced at her tablet and tapped something into her keyboard. When she'd finished, she sat very still for at least ten seconds with her fingers steepled, just looking at me, her eyes slightly narrowed. I hoped she wasn't going to ask me anything awkward about why I'd messed up.

'So.' She smiled. 'How did you feel about your experience, Amber?'

'The VR?' My breath caught. I'd loved it, even if it had left me dazed and confused, but I guessed she wanted a more articulate answer than that. Before I could carry on though, she fluttered a hand airily, making her gold bracelet flash, and continued in her smooth, confident voice:

'It's remarkable technology, Amber. Ingenious and quite breathtaking in its capabilities. VR has come a long way, although it can certainly be destabilizing if one isn't used to it.' She paused, and her dark-blue eyes bored into me with an intensity that made me feel like I was the most important person in the world. 'How do you think you did?'

I took a deep breath.

'Badly? I mean, I *failed*, didn't I? The gameplay felt smooth though. But once both targets entered the shop, it got tricky. There wasn't much room. Maybe I'd do better if I had another go?'

She drained her coffee. 'Well, your performance was far from bad. In fact, categorically, it was the opposite.' Her eyes sparkled and I noticed a gap in between her top teeth; it suited her.

The floor squeaked and the tiles slid open, in the same way that the wall panels had. A small pillar rose up with a glass of lemonade on it. She must have ordered my drink from her tablet. Now that *was* cool.

'A bigger failure would have been if you'd blown your cover. It's true you didn't manage to take a photograph, but your *cover* stayed intact. You didn't put yourself, or anyone else, at risk. Very smart, I'd say. Tell me, what do you think about EZ? What we're doing?' She reached forward and handed me the glass of lemonade.

'The company seems up on all the latest tech, that's for sure.'

'Yes, we are.' She sat back again. 'We're creating a training programme. You weren't a failure at all. Sometimes, in the world of espionage, it's more prudent to play the long game.'

The world of espionage? I wouldn't go that far, Alex Rider.

There was a small silence before she leaned forward, so close that I could see the faint hairs on her upper lip.

'Right.' I gave her a look that said, *And so what?* I downed half my lemonade, watching the column sink slowly back into the floor and the tiles close up again.

The long game—what was she on about? The lemonade had given me brain freeze. 'Am I missing something?'

'Amber. To succeed in the real-world version of your VR experience, you'd need to weigh up risks in a variety of situations. You need an ability to make snap decisions—trusting your instinct is imperative.'

I was confused. *The real-world version?*

'Are you still talking about gameplay?'

She threw back her head and burst into deep laughter. 'Oh! The gameplay? That's merely our front, dear. Our cover. EZ doesn't exist. Well, not as you know it. There is no escape room, or ongoing research into teenagers' leisure activities and habits.'

My blood ran cold. *What the—?*

She shifted forward again. 'Oh, don't worry,

Amber. We are a *real* organization. We have a genuine interest in you personally.'

Suddenly, Mum's warnings about 'talking to strangers' shot into my brain and my heart thudded. Instinctively, my hand patted my pocket for my mobile. *Good*. Now, which wall panels would I need to touch to get out of here? Were they fingerprint-coded?

'You're interested in me personally, because . . . ?' I asked, a trickle of ice inching its way down my spine. My hand tightened around my glass. Could I hurl it if I needed to? What if my lemonade had been . . . drugged? How would I ever get out, the door had no handle! *Keep calm, Amber. Don't show your fear.*

'Because we believe you have what it takes.' She attempted a reassuring smile. 'My name is Clara. I work for The Agency. We specialize in global espionage.'

If this was a joke, I wasn't laughing.

'Ha. Good one.' I nodded. 'You almost fooled me there! Did Vi put you up to this?'

'Amber.' Clara's voice suddenly sounded stern, just like my headmistress. 'We are spies and we're in need of teen recruits. We'd like you to come and work for us.'

CHAPTER 5

As I sat in the back of the car Clara had ordered to
take me home, driving away from what I'd thought
was Escape Zone but . . . wasn't, I ran through the
whole crazy scene in my head again. Clara's words
were spinning around my brain like bumper cars.

The rest of our 'meeting' had been spent with
Clara firing questions at me as if I was being
interrogated. Some of the questions were easy to
answer: yes, I loved the kick of the VR game. Yes,
I'd wanted to succeed and had been disappointed
when I'd failed. Yes, I was pretty sure where I'd gone
wrong and why. Yes, I enjoyed my own company. Yes,
I could keep a secret. That one obviously reminded
me of Vi, and us drifting away from each other, and
her latching on to Taylor. I also thought of Mum's
pregnancy and how I was keeping *that* from Vi, the

person I thought would be my best friend forever.

Other questions Clara asked me weren't so easy. Would I do whatever it took to achieve my goal as a spy? I had no idea. I was honest about that, but Clara just nodded, like my answer didn't faze her.

'You impressed us, Amber,' she'd said. 'You evidently take on challenges with a positive attitude. You *want* to succeed. That, coupled with your propensity for strategic thinking, means you have the perfect mindset for what we need. Your confidence needs a boost and you ought to give yourself more credit. But your self-deprecating humour makes you likeable and human: excellent traits for a spy who needs to blend in effectively.'

She beamed at me like I'd made her the happiest person alive before adding, 'You stood out during your escape-room test yesterday, demonstrating leadership qualities and keeping a level head under pressure. All of that is why we invited you in today.'

I'd frowned, trying to catch up with everything she'd just said.

'But how exactly do you know so much about me, Clara?'

'We've been watching you. We know you're physically fit. One of our team has observed that your performance at school on the running track is excellent. Well-paced and full of stamina; while others shoot forward because they're impatient, you keep the end objective in mind. You think things through before acting. You're observant. Do you understand how rare those qualities are in teenagers?' She gave a throaty laugh.

Wow—that was quite some stalking The Agency had been doing! I didn't know whether to be impressed or terrified; maybe both. Clara had looked down at her tablet, and then looked back up at me.

'Due to your parents registering you with a donor card, we have legal access to your medical records.' She smiled, as though this wasn't disturbing information. 'You're a picture of health. Your bloodwork and immune system are top notch. And of course, the fact that you're way above average height and weight for your age is a distinct advantage, allowing you to pass for three, or even four, years older if necessary.'

'Right. OK. Um . . . good to know?' I sat there, stunned. Finding out that a complete stranger knew everything about me was *very weird*. How would she like it if her privacy had been invaded? But I tried to focus on the positives. She was right, I didn't get colds very often, and I came from a family with a longer than average lifespan (both sets of grandparents were alive and well)—unless I got run over by a truck or maimed by an assassin ...

At that point a shot of fear went through me, but I shook it off, and told myself that encountering an assassin was highly unlikely . . . Probably?

They wanted me because I had skillz. *I could do this*. I'd always been nosy—aged six, I'd had deep suspicions about the Tooth Fairy and the Easter Bunny. Under my interrogation techniques, Mum and Dad both folded in five minutes flat and confessed all. And she was right, I was observant; always noticed when Vi or any teachers changed anything about themselves.

'So . . .' Clara had interrupted my thoughts. 'I think we're ready to start.' Then she handed me a state-of-the-art mobile, telling me it was pre-programmed with the details I'd need. I'd never seen anything so cute! Teeny-tiny and closed in on itself like a clamshell. (My own phone was Mum's cast-off.) Clara assured me it was shockproof, waterproof, and drop-proof. I kind of wanted to test this, but I didn't. Apparently, this phone was how The Agency would reach me and I had to keep it with me at all times.

Sitting in the car now, I caught the eye of the driver,

then looked away. I *knew* I wasn't dreaming. That meeting had actually happened!

The clam phone vibrated in my hand. I opened my fist, stared at it in shock, like I'd never seen a phone before. I opened it and touched the envelope on screen.

`Welcome, Amber. Any questions, please don't hesitate to get in touch. We think you'll be an invaluable member of the team.`

I put it into my pocket, grinning. *Invaluable?* Excellent! I could get used to this. I'd spent the last year not believing in myself much and when you do that for long enough then you start to convince everyone else of it, too. But deep down I'd always hoped I was special, and I'd really felt it during the escape-room experience. The buzz I'd got from getting us out of there, thinking quicker than everyone else and noticing things that passed them by. I might not be a grade-A student, but here was proof I wasn't a complete loser either.

But what did I know about spies? Um . . . *nothing*. OK, maybe that wasn't true. I'd watched some *James Bond* and *Mission Impossible* films with Dad on lazy Sunday afternoons. I expected gadgets, but . . . DEATH, too. High-risk car chases, casinos, exotic locations, aeroplanes, lasers, villains with cats, and

. . . oh yeah, did I mention DEATH?

Jeez. What had I got myself into? This wasn't a game! I could probably still back out and say thanks but no thanks . . . but Clara had mentioned travel, disguises, and learning new skills and . . . it sounded so thrilling and cool and . . . *way more interesting* than school.

If I said no to this opportunity, then maybe I'd never get another experience like it. But it was too overwhelming; I needed advice. But how could I get that if I couldn't tell anyone!

I willed myself to relax. *Chill, Amber.*

I'd wait till I got home. Go to my room and make a list of 'pros' and 'cons'. Lists always helped. It was reassuring seeing things written down in black and white.

'Um, excuse me,' I said, leaning forward as far as my seatbelt would allow and tapping on the glass partition separating me and the driver.

The glass inched down with a whirring noise. 'Yes? May I help you?'

His accent was thick, as if his tongue was too wide for his mouth. *Russian? Polish, maybe?*

'I know Clara told you where to drop me off, but the thing is, if anyone sees this car, there'll be more questions than answers, you know? Just by the park would be great, if you don't mind. Less . . . *obvious*.'

He didn't reply, just nodded. With another whir, the glass rolled back up.

My watch said it was nearly seven. Mum would be serving dinner any minute. I checked my normal phone, not my spy one, and *gah!* I'd switched it off while in Spy HQ . . .

As I suspected, I had three missed calls from Mum and a bunch of texts from Vi.

Still at EZ? Why is your phone off?

Having fun?

You OK? Your mum texted me 5 mins ago FOR THE SECOND TIME. Didn't you tell her where you were going? I covered for you, said you were in the loo at mine!

That last one was only sent ten minutes ago— not a massive disaster. We slowly drove along the road parallel to mine, until we approached the small playground Vi and I used to hang out at.

The driver pulled alongside the kerb and I hopped out. He rolled the window down.

'My name is Alexei,' he said, with a toothy grin. 'See you soon, Amber.'

'Thanks, Alexei.' I nodded goodbye.

The front door slammed louder than I'd meant it to.

'Amber?' Mum emerged from the kitchen, a tea towel over her shoulder. 'Seriously, love, if you're going to be late, you *must* keep your phone on. You *know* that!'

'Sorry, Mum. Vi wanted me to try out for this drama thing after school and then we went to hers, but I was *desperate* for the loo. I think . . . I had too much spag bol last night? My stomach was, you know, really *upset*.'

I'd come up with this excuse in the twenty seconds it had taken me to walk to our front door. Thinking on my feet like Clara had said. I was impressed with myself.

I turned away from Mum's keen gaze and fiddled with the straps on my backpack.

'Oh, poor you. Want me to get you something for it?' She tried to lean in and kiss my cheek, but I was still feeling strange about the Baby news, so I pulled away.

'Still feel ropey . . .' I murmured, which I hoped stopped her feelings being hurt.

'Anyway.' Mum looked cheery. 'The midwife appointment went well. The baby is fine and growing—'

'Uh-oh. I need to go again!' I grabbed my bag, dashed upstairs and straight into the toilet.

'What about dinner?' she called after me.

'Not hungry!' I yelled back.

Excellent, Amber. Mission to avoid interrogation and unwanted pregnancy updates accomplished!

I felt good and bad at the same time. But I had so much to think about, and I wasn't ready to talk Baby. Not yet.

I waited in the bathroom for a few minutes and then dashed across the landing to my room, closing the door behind me. I leaned against it, finally starting to relax. When my bedroom door was closed, it was as good as being locked.

I loved my room. This morning over breakfast Mum suggested it could become the baby's nursery and asked what I thought about a loft conversion. I was hurt when she'd said I could move into the attic. She made out it was all about the baby being noisy and me not getting disturbed. 'Having your own stairs will be like a private hideaway!' she'd said.

I admit, that did *sound* cool, but it would be strange being on a different floor to everyone else. I couldn't help but feel that I was being inched out, or hidden away, like that mad woman in the attic we'd read about in *Jane Eyre*.

My stomach gurgled; I was starving. I dragged my lunchbox out of my backpack. Half a bagel and a half-melted KitKat finger that I hadn't had time to eat earlier. *Yes!*

Sitting on my bed, chewing, I thought over what Clara had said. It all made sense in a funny way. Why *not* use teenagers as spies? Who'd ever suspect us? Our reputation with the general public was often negative, anyway. People writing us off as sullen, selfish or self-obsessed, without taking the time to get to know us.

Hopefully, I'd just signed up for the biggest adventure of my entire life! Now *I* was the one with a secret.

My phone buzzed. 'Hi Vi.'

'Alright? So, what happened? Why didn't you tell your mum what you were doing? How was Escape Zone? Were Connor and Milly there again?' She fired questions at me.

I had no idea what to tell her.

I held the phone next to my ear for so long without saying anything that Vi started going, 'Hello? Amber? Can you hear me?'

I wanted to squeal and tell her everything. She'd love to hear about Clara and would go nuts for the whole spy thing, but I'd been sworn to secrecy. I wasn't in the habit of lying to my best friend, though. The only way out of this was to downplay everything and make it sound rubbish. That way she wouldn't feel like she'd missed out and might stop asking questions. Oh, and I'd ask her about herself, too; nothing like a little misdirection.

'No, they weren't there. It was pretty . . . boring? I had to fill out a bunch of questionnaires. What did you get up to?'

'Actually, Layla came over.'

Layla? Taylor-the-bully's sidekick. 'How come?' I said, trying to keep my voice light and supremely *un*bothered.

'I've got this big maths assessment coming up. She was helping me with some equations.'

I felt a stab of jealousy. 'I can help you with maths.'

'Amber, you're in the top set! I don't have the first clue what you're doing. Anyway, even though she's a bit of an airhead, she's good at explaining stuff.'

'Oh. Right.' I'd never heard of Layla going around to Vi's house before. The hot feeling intensified in my chest. 'How was it?'

'Well . . .' And then Vi paused in a way that made my stomach sink. Whatever she was going to say next, I wasn't sure I wanted to hear it.

'She came round, and then the weirdest thing happened.'

Sure. This was my cue to inquire further. Vi

always did this when she wanted me to probe.

'Which was?' I prompted.

'Taylor showed up like ten minutes later!'

'Really?'

'Really.'

I couldn't stop myself from sounding bitchy. 'What, and you just happened to invite her in?'

Now I *was* properly mad. Taylor was a bully, plain and simple. She hadn't bothered me since primary school, but neither of us liked her. Her parents were well off and her dad worked abroad a lot, and all she ever talked about was what they'd bought her and which fancy holidays she was going on. She often missed school and was always getting detentions. Last year she'd got into trouble for trolling someone online.

Was Vi heading towards that group? I couldn't believe it. I left her alone once after school and there she was, fraternizing with the enemy.

'Yeah. Look. It was fine. She's changed since primary school. Really. She's not that bad.'

My hand tightened around the phone. *Grr!* No way could I listen to Vi telling me that Taylor was alright. I'd had a great day and my happy feelings were slipping away listening to this crap.

'If you say so. Vi, I have to go, Mum's calling. See

you tomorrow.'

Buzzzzzzzzzzz. I'd just managed to drift off after my argument with Vi when something vibrated next to my ear or . . . *inside it?*

I jerked awake, convinced a wasp had found its way into my room. Then I remembered. My hand shot under the pillow for the spy phone and I flipped it open.

Residential training, this weekend. Details to follow. Everything taken care of.

CHAPTER 6

The next morning, Mum was in her dressing gown at the kitchen table sipping tea, squinting at a piece of paper. Next to her was a copy of *Mother and Baby* magazine. *Already?*

'Morning! Why didn't you tell me about this?' she asked, waving the paper around.

I felt my stomach contract but tried to play it cool.

'Erm . . . tell you 'bout what?' I rubbed my eyes, indicating I was barely awake.

'I'm so proud of you, Amber!' Mum's eyes were blurry with tears, and I tried to glimpse the words on the paper. It looked official. My stomach tightened further. Who'd written to my parents? Clara? I thought everything was Top Secret. How could it have been that fast?

'Aw Mum, that's always nice to hear, but . . .'

'You scored in the top five per cent on their STEM tests,' Mum clarified. 'And for this special training weekend, they've only selected the *outstanding* candidates . . .' She paused. 'How come we didn't know you were in the running?'

Mentally, I ran through various excuses. 'I didn't mention it because . . . I didn't want to let you down. You know, in case I didn't get through?' I shrugged, smiling: universal teen for 'no biggie'.

'I did the tests *ages* ago,' I added. 'Can I just check the letter to jog my memory?'

Mum handed the letter over and I skimmed it, expressionless. The Agency had arranged the training weekend and sold it as an academic opportunity. *Smart.* I recognized senior staff names from school who'd been copied in. *Wow.* These guys were good; they had people everywhere.

'I'll help you pack after school,' Mum said. 'You'll need an early night if you're going to be studying all weekend.'

Mum's enthusiasm stung a little. Last year it took ages to persuade her to let me go on a school residential trip, but now, apparently, she couldn't wait to get rid of me. I bet she wanted to make Baby plans with Dad without me getting in the way. This wasn't about me at all; it was about her.

Keep a lid on it, Amber.

The front doorbell rang: Vi calling to walk to school.

I grabbed a piece of toast sticking up out of the toaster. 'I can go then?'

'Of course!' Mum cried. 'You're such a clever girl. *So* proud of you.' She stood up with her arms outstretched. Suddenly, I didn't feel that proud of myself.

I nearly hugged her then, because she looked like she meant it, but instead I ducked out of her embrace and rushed to the door with the toast jammed in my mouth.

'Sorry about last night, Vi,' I said, closing the front door behind me. 'I felt so drained after EZ. Thanks for covering.'

She shrugged. 'Whatever.'

'And Mum was . . .' I bit my lip. 'Giving me a hard time about being late and . . . you know.'

Vi's expression softened. 'Don't worry about it,' she said. 'You know, I probably only even invited Layla over because I felt . . . left out.'

I pointed at her sparkly studs. 'Are those new earrings?'

'Like them?' Vi touched her ears. 'You're the only

one who's even noticed.'

'They're cute.'

Vi shifted her bag up on her shoulder. 'Taylor gave them to me.'

'That's . . . pretty random.' But that was how Taylor worked, buying people's friendships. Why couldn't Vi see through her?

'I know, right? Anyway, how was yesterday, *really?* You barely said anything last night.'

'It wasn't much fun without you,' I said.

Partly true.

'Really?' Her face brightened.

I opened my mouth to make her feel better and lies poured out. 'It was basically a waste of time. You *really* didn't miss anything.'

Vi's entire face lit up and I knew I'd said the right thing, though I wasn't looking forward to delivering my next massive dose of disappointment.

'So. Tom's party this weekend?' Vi hopped about, excited. 'Mum's hired a magician. I absolutely can't deal with such lameness on my own. I thought you could stay over.'

I clenched my jaw and stared ahead as we walked.

'Saturday will be stuffing party bags and planning games. Then, the party madness starts at 2 p.m. on Sunday. But at least you'll get a lie-in.'

How to begin the let-down process? 'Vi? I can't . . . I'm really sorry but I won't be able to come round on Saturday.'

'Oh.' She couldn't meet my gaze and glanced down at her phone. 'Well. I guess I can handle party bags by myself. Is 2 p.m. on Sunday OK?'

'Not Sunday either.' I cringed and pulled a face.

'No!' She looked up from her phone. 'Why not?'

'I've been invited to this . . . thing.'

What was I going to say? Quick!

'What *thing*?' She narrowed her eyes, looking suspicious. 'Another EZ day?' she asked with a pout.

I shook my head. 'No, no. EZ is finished. This is . . . a school thing?' I finished lamely, cringing at my own doubtful tone.

She huffed. '*What* school thing?'

'An intro to STEM for girls.'

'You what?' She wrinkled her nose and all her freckles merged.

'Science, technology, engineering, and maths, you know. Mr Grafton has been giving me extra homew—'

'*What?* You're going into school this weekend?' She put her hand on my arm. 'Poor you! But it's not all day, right?'

'Actually . . . it's a residential weekend at a

61

different school, miles away. I have to stay over. Mum's *really* into it.'

Vi stared hard at me, waiting for more, but I had nothing. 'Won't I see you then?' she said quietly.

We'd organized Tom's parties for years and always had a brilliant time. This was a Big Deal. Briefly, I considered telling Clara this wasn't a good time . . . but then, when *would* be? Vi and I always had weekend plans. Anyway, the truth was, I wanted to be away from home for a while. And I was curious too, dying to know what spy training actually involved.

I threw my arm round Vi's shoulders and pulled her close to me. 'Sorry old bean!'

'Tom will be gutted.' Vi's expression grew guarded again. 'Why didn't you mention it before?'

'I only just found out. I was on the reserve list. Someone from another school dropped out last minute. Besides . . . I knew you'd call me *nerdy*!'

Her lips twitched, and for a second I thought we were OK, and she was going to laugh, but then her mouth tightened again.

'Whatever,' she said carelessly. 'No worries. Layla said she'd help me out, if I needed support. I can't organize a party for twelve kids by myself, and Mum's working, so . . . putting up with Layla's a small price to pay. Did you know Taylor has twin stepbrothers? They're nine. Maybe I should invite them . . .'

Vi rummaged in her bag for some gum, not looking at me. My heart was hammering in my chest. I couldn't believe it—she knew how I felt about Taylor. But this was my fault. I swallowed back the tears prickling my eyes.

'Sorry, Vi,' I said again. 'I'm such a bad friend right now. I'll make it up to you and Tom. Maybe we can go bowling and spoil him?'

Vi looked up from scrolling through her phone and a tiny smile appeared.

'He'd love that,' she said softly. 'If you add in playing Lego then he'll definitely forgive you. Just . . . maybe don't make promises you can't keep, Amber? That really is the worst.'

As she turned to walk ahead through the school gates, my shoulders slumped. I was losing count of all the lies I'd told over the past twenty-four hours.

I put my hand into my coat pocket and my fingers brushed the spy phone. I trembled—it could buzz any moment.

I hoped The Agency had a beginner's manual on how to navigate this spy business properly: things were getting . . . complicated.

CHAPTER 7

In the same car as before, Alexei pressed buttons on the dashboard and the windows blacked out, going smoky. I could see out but, he assured me, no one could see in. I felt like a film star as we travelled to the training weekend. Did people think someone important was driving past? In just one week I'd been catapulted into a completely different life. How could things change so quickly?

My stomach flipped. I wanted to do this, but I was nervous too. I'm pretty shy around new people, whereas Vi is Little Miss Sociable, always making friends easily. Vi skirts the edges of any 'popular crowd'; loves singing and dancing and drama classes. I'd normally have my head in a book. I'd literally melt if you put me on stage in front of an audience.

Maybe I *should* join the drama group with Vi,

although I'd hate every second of it. But then at least Layla—and worse, Taylor!—wouldn't take my place, and me and Vi would be as close as we've always been . . .

I swallowed. I'd get through this weekend first, then I could tackle the Vi situation, and find a way of telling her about Mum's pregnancy.

As we drove, I opened the tiny cupboard in front of me and took out a packet of honey-roasted cashews. Munching, I thought about Mum sending me off this morning, barely a tear in her eye. What would she and Dad do this weekend? Move into Babies R Us?

The Agency obviously had connections all over. At school, by the time I'd had my first lesson, they'd emailed my parents a full schedule of my non-existent STEM activities, and copied me in, explaining that the school encouraged teens to switch off mobiles, in order to foster concentration and practise non-reliance on social media.

Smart. Whose parents wouldn't love that?

Mum and Dad had been asked to call or email only in an emergency.

For over an hour, Alexei drove further into the countryside. Roads with houses gave way to fields that stretched for miles. The roads became windy and narrow, and the hedges higher.

Eventually, the car turned into an empty field with a warehouse-type building in the middle of it, but judging by the weeds growing through jagged, broken windows, this couldn't be the place. It was completely abandoned.

Alexei turned off the engine and I listened to the clicking and whirring of it cooling down. For an insane moment, my heart slammed in my chest— why hadn't I asked for any directions, or an address? What if this was an elaborate scam and I'd been brought here to be chopped up into a billion pieces? My eyes scanned around for anything I could use to defend myself, if needed. *Ooh*: a bottle opener.

Alexei lowered the glass partition, turned in his seat and smiled. 'We are here, Miss.'

'Where are we?' I asked, trying to keep my breathing under control.

'Miss? Step out of the car now, please.'

What would be outside to greet me? I pocketed the bottle opener.

Hooking my backpack over my shoulder, I opened the door and swung my feet round to land on gravel. The car drove off at speed, kicking up so much dust I had to step back and shield my eyes.

I wouldn't consider myself a suspicious or

nervous person, but once again, thoughts galloped around my overactive imagination—maybe this spy stuff wasn't real. If I *wasn't* about to be buried out here, or held for ransom, then at the very least I was being secretly filmed for some YouTube hoax.

The sun reflected off the building's broken windows about ten metres from where I stood. *Where was I?* The middle of nowhere in a barren, deserted landscape.

We'd driven for over an hour. How far had we travelled? What had Alexei's average speed been? As I calculated distances, a mechanical whirring noise started up behind me and I swear the ground underneath me shuddered.

What looked like a cracked paving slab shifted and the ground slid open. Out of this space rose a square concrete platform encased in clear plastic on a thick, metal pillar. And standing on it, grinning as if I was the funniest sight she'd ever seen, was Clara. Head to toe in silver. She suited every colour.

'Well,' she said, smooth as butter, as the plastic tube swung open. 'Come along now, you can't stand there gawking. One never knows how far CHAOS's surveillance reaches.'

What?

Clara edged to one side and I gingerly stepped

onto the small platform; we ended up practically pressed against each other. She activated a tiny remote control and the tube closed, the platform slowly descending.

'Bulletproof,' she said, indicating the clear plastic.

Staring upwards, I watched the paving slab slide back over, making us disappear again. The temperature suddenly dropped as we headed underground. I shivered.

Oh, my giddy aunt, as Mum said when she was trying not to swear. A sharp thrill fluttered in my chest. This was the coolest thing ever!

The platform settled with a clunk, the tube opened, and we stepped out directly onto a wide glass balcony with railings all around it. Spread out below us was a cavernous entrance hall, and leading off it, five dark, long tunnels, like tentacles, connecting the biggest rabbit warren ever. There were pipes and wires, panels of lights, buttons and switches everywhere. The eerie hum of electric lights buzzed.

'Welcome!' Clara grasped the railing lightly, surveying her spy kingdom.

'Um, is it just us here?' I asked, nervously. I couldn't see anyone else. We were deep underground and this balcony was very high up. What if Clara tripped and fell? I'd be trapped down here!

'No. There are two security guards, two technicians, and Iyabo, your trainer. They've worked with me for years. On occasion, I've trusted them with my life—literally. You're in safe hands. Come.'

I followed her as she talked, the pathways lighting up as we passed through a network of tunnels and glass-fronted rooms. I had to keep my mouth from dropping open, because I'd never seen so much sparkling glass and glittering metal before. It was as if I'd been catapulted into a shiny future of robots and tech.

'Over the next two days, we have a lot to cover but we'll ensure some downtime is built in, too. I've programmed the iPad in your room with your favourite films and music—'

'How—?'

'We know your social media habits. As I said, we've been monitoring your . . . tastes.'

'Oh, right.' Yeah. *Still freaky as heck.*

'Your room is equipped with a king-size bed, walk-in-wardrobe, TV, sound system and a wet room. I'm afraid you shan't be able to go online, due to the risk of being traced. I'm sure you understand. Besides, I can assure you, you'll be far too exhausted to miss scrolling through HappySnap.'

A weekend with no internet access? This had better be worth it.

A secret underground hidden-to-the-world spy training bunker was the oddest place I'd ever woken up in on a Saturday morning.

My Saturdays usually involved homework, cross-country training, seeing Vi, a film with Mum or Dad, and maybe a takeaway. Usual stuff that any fourteen-year-old might do. Now though, I had no idea what to expect. My tummy tingled in anticipation.

My room had no windows—one wall was a massive mirror, and the other three were a changing kaleidoscope of outside scenery, accessible via a remote-control wall panel (I chose a forest setting). But the low ceiling and calming blue lights made it somehow feel cosy too.

I was lying on the comfortable bed, flicking through the iPad, when suddenly, a panel in the ceiling opened and a navy jumpsuit on a padded hanger came down on a long, thin wire.

I sat up quickly, blinking. Leaning forward, I unhooked the hanger and peered at the jumpsuit. No label. I stretched it out with my hands. The material was slightly rubbery; like a wetsuit, but lighter and softer. A shiver went through me. *My spy uniform!*

Better get ready for action.

The bathroom was bigger than our kitchen at home. Sleek metal, chrome, and glass everywhere. The shower was powerful and the luxury soaps and shampoo lining the shower tray made me feel like I was in a hotel.

As the water poured over me, I had to tell myself this was really happening. I wasn't dreaming!

I hadn't given much thought to spies before now. Who would? I knew governments protected themselves, and the people they governed, and that countries had secrets. But that was all. Thinking about it now though, I guessed more went on behind the scenes than most people realized as they carried on with their regular lives.

And here I was, entering this world of secrets. But I couldn't tell a soul.

Usually, if anything remotely exciting happened, I told people. Did it even exist unless it was on social media? My grandparents and parents sometimes talked about their teenage years: no smartphones, Netflix or Amazon. Waiting a week to watch an episode of a TV show would drive me crazy! I had to admit, though, after a few hours without my phone, it was kind of nice not worrying about my 'likes' or messages. Instead of feeling I needed to constantly check in, in case I missed any school drama, I had space to think and breathe. It was like being on holiday.

Clara had made it clear that I'd have to keep secrets from *everyone but authorized personnel*. Not only keep secrets, but lie, too. I'd told a few white lies, obviously, but proper lies? I wasn't sure if I could handle deceit on that level. Hopefully, I'd be given tips and techniques while I was here.

As I turned off the shower and slipped into a fluffy bathrobe, I thought of Vi. I wish Vi had been recruited as a spy too; it'd be fun to experience this together. She'd love it here; it was so stylish. The glass didn't steam up, the towel rails and floor were heated; everything was luxurious.

I walked past the mirrored wall and lights sparkled as sensors picked up my footsteps. I took off my robe and stepped into my navy jumpsuit, and it fitted perfectly, with room to move.

As I was drying my hair, my spy phone buzzed and lit up. Clara's face appeared onscreen and I pressed the speakerphone icon.

'Amber?'

I moved into eyeshot. 'Hi, Clara.'

'I trust you've settled in? I've an important matter to take care of now, so you won't see much of me, but

I'll swing by later to administer the lie detector test. You'll be in Iyabo's capable hands. She's schooled in Krav Maga, Wing Chun and Brazilian jiu-jitsu.'

'Jiu-jitsu? I'll be fighting?'

The only time I'd ever been in a fight was the first day of secondary school. Taylor had mocked the picture of Marie Curie in my locker and when she ripped it in half, I put chewing gum in her hair and . . . well, the less said about that, the better.

'Naturally, violence should be avoided,' Clara said. 'Iyabo will explain. You'll focus on self-defence and how to keep your cover. There'll be tests, too. When you're ready, do come on up. Breakfast is laid out for you.'

CHAPTER 8

In a room painted a soothing, pale peach, with one mirrored wall (was I being watched?), The Agency had laid out an incredible breakfast buffet.

My stomach was jittery, and I barely managed half a bagel. I'd hoped other teen spies would have arrived by now, but so far, it'd been *very* quiet. I pushed my bagel aside and picked at some strawberries instead.

'Amber? I'm Iyabo.'

I choked on my orange juice and turned to see a tall, slim black woman smiling with her hand held out. She was dressed in a similar jumpsuit to mine, except hers was red. Her hair was in thick braids curled on her head and fixed with a purple headscarf.

'Hi,' I said shyly, shaking her hand. 'Iya—'

'It's pronounced Iy-YAA-bow,' she explained. 'I'm Nigerian.' She scooped up a handful of blueberries.

'Ooh, you don't mind, do you? Right. Are you ready to begin?'

'I'm ready,' I squeaked.

'No need to be nervous. Hopefully Clara explained I'll take good care of you.'

I relaxed a little. Iyabo looked only a few years older than me. She perched on the end of the table. '*I* always feel better when I know what's expected of me. Do you know what I mean?'

'Yep.' I nodded, relieved. 'Me too.'

'OK. So, our plan this morning is various tests, focusing on self-defence skills.'

'And this afternoon?'

'Surveillance and investigative tests.'

'Are *you* a spy too?' I whispered.

'I don't do much field work.' She leaned in closer to me. 'My background is cognitive psychology,' she whispered back. We shared a grin.

'Cognitive . . . what's that?'

'Psychology focusing on thinking, intelligence, and memory. All the mental processes which underlie our behaviour. As you can imagine, very useful for espionage. I also teach martial arts to new recruits and ensure recruits who've been with us for years don't lose their touch and are kept up to date with the latest fighting methods.'

'Cool!' I couldn't help saying it out loud.

Iyabo nodded. 'I've been practising jiu-jitsu for years now.' She paused. 'Have you got siblings?' she asked.

I shook my head. *For now, anyway.*

'Well, my older sister and I never got on,' Iyabo said. 'She was a real bully. My father loved martial arts, so we'd watch films together and when I saw Michelle Yeoh and Maggie Q . . . I begged to learn something similar. I've done various martial arts ever since I was your age. You're fourteen, right?'

'Yeah.'

'The fact you're so tall makes you look much older. Undeniably an advantage for The Agency. Clara says you run?' We got up from the table and Iyabo guided me through the dining area along a smooth walkway, like an airport travelator. 'Sprinting, or long distance?'

'Long distance.'

'Great. You'll have stamina then.'

'Iyabo? This probably sounds stupid, but ...' I trailed off, embarrassed that I didn't even know the basics of what I was getting into.

'Anything you ask is not, under *any* circumstances, stupid. Fire away.'

'I've heard of MI5 and MI6 as spy places, but

which one is this part of?'

'Neither. We're actually more involved with the UN, but we operate independently really.'

United Nations. Promoting peace? I liked the sound of that.

We arrived at a small gym, which looked oddly primitive: four tractor tyres, two thick ropes, a treadmill, and a bench with dumb-bells.

Iyabo tested my heart rate while she made me run a steady mile followed by a sprint on the treadmill, and afterwards took my blood pressure. Then we moved on to another room, which was blindingly white, like a high-tech doctor's office.

Here, Iyabo took my vitals: a blood test and a full 3-D body scan. While I stepped into the chamber and stood being scanned by lasers, I wondered if there would be any fun parts to the training or if I was here alone with only two adults for company the entire weekend.

'Try and remain still,' said Iyabo through an earpiece, as I twitched while thinking. 'The scanner captures a 3-D image of your entire body in one sweep. The tech is new, an advanced version of the MRI scanners that hospitals have. Ready?'

'Think so,' I said, wondering when the mental testing would happen. Surely they'd recruited me for my brains too?

A beeping noise like an alarm clock sounded, and the door panel hissed open. I stepped out. 'Will I get sent the results? I'd like to see my insides.'

Iyabo laughed. 'Weirdo! OK, I'll let Clara know. Now, I think we're ready for the fun stuff.'

I grinned. 'Oh, good! I mean, not to say this hasn't been fun, but . . .'

'I know, I know. Come on.'

Iyabo's warm, calm nature made me feel at ease. She led me through a maze of narrow corridors heading deeper underground, if that was possible. This place stretched for miles. We passed shiny metal doors (all closed) and eventually reached an open area, like my school gym. The floor was spongy, as if thick yoga mats were under my feet.

'What do you know about self-defence?' she asked, hands on hips.

'Um, *run*?'

'That's one strategy,' Iyabo nodded, smiling. 'But it's not always practical, right? For me, self-defence is more about using strength and skill, not aggression, to defend yourself if under attack. Against my sister I used Krav Maga and Wing Chun. They're tactical defence systems designed to quickly neutralize threats and are *especially* good for women because you don't have to rely on brute strength. Krav Maga is effective, but not . . . graceful. Aim for your attacker's eyes, face, throat, neck, groin, and fingers: the vulnerable spots. Wing Chun is about attacking and defending at the same time. Deadly if you're close enough.'

A shudder rushed up my legs. 'I don't need to be deadly, do I?' I yelped.

Iyabo smiled but didn't respond. Instead, she took off the pouch wrapped around her waist. 'Now.' She planted her feet firmly on the ground. 'Krav Maga is based around your own natural reactions about being alert and avoiding sticky situations in the first place. We'll focus on the basic moves. OK?'

'OK.' Standing opposite her, I copied her pose.

Suddenly, she lunged and tumbled me to the ground in a headlock. *Ow!* My face and cheek were mashed into the mat. I couldn't breathe. I panted shallowly. This *hurt. Really hurt!* Tears sprang to my eyes. She didn't stop pushing, and I started to see stars.

Just as I wondered if I was about to pass out, Iyabo yanked me up as if I were no heavier than a rag doll.

'The open-hand strike: use the heel of your hand to aim for the eyes or nose. *Don't* pull your arm back, otherwise your attacker knows what's coming.

Keep your arm and elbow tight into your chest, and *then* strike.'

I leapt forward but she easily ducked out of the way, light on her feet.

'You've seen pictures of snakes lashing out? Be that snake. Keep your elbow up!'

I tried again. 'This is tough!'

'Slow down. *Focus.*' Iyabo's tone was encouraging, but firm.

I tried again and again but kept pulling my arm back. I must have done the same move fifty times and I was getting sweaty. I was too clumsy. Mum says teenagers can be awkward because they're growing so fast, but Vi didn't bang into doorframes, or trip over her own feet, as often as I did. I was going to have work hard at this.

Iyabo was so nimble. The second my foot lifted off the ground, or I raised my knee, she neatly avoided me.

'Step forward,' she instructed.

I did, crying out when she twisted my arm behind my back. Gently, yet effortlessly, she tumbled me again. *Wow.* On my back, staring at the ceiling, with a camera's red light blinking, I wondered how the heck that had just happened.

Seriously, what had I got myself into?

CHAPTER 9

An hour later I was totally exhausted and was staring at the ceiling *again* after being flipped for the hundredth time.

'That'll do,' said Iyabo with a grin.

I stood up, dusting myself down. Then I took a long drink from the water fountain in the corner and splashed water onto my burning cheeks. Maybe I wasn't cut out for this after all.

'Catch your breath and we'll head to the other testing area,' said Iyabo. 'You did well, Amber, but you need to immerse yourself in the practice. Soon it should come naturally. Please, don't get discouraged. Practice is key.'

I seriously hoped I could believe her.

'Right.' Iyabo held out her arm, gesturing to a door across the room. 'We're done with the physical stuff for now. Let's move on.'

I followed her, thoughts swirling through my brain again. There was so much to learn, and I wasn't convinced I'd ever master it.

In the next room, Iyabo told me to take a seat at a table with a laptop on it. I sat in the spinning office chair and felt cheerier again. When me and Vi used to visit my dad's office, we'd spin ourselves in the chairs till we felt dizzy; this took me to my happy place. I wondered how Vi's party-bag-stuffing was going and hoped that Taylor wasn't round her house.

Before I could travel too far down that mental one-way street, Clara walked in carrying a clipboard, elegant as always.

She smiled at us both. 'How has the morning treated you so far, Amber?'

I spun around in my chair, lifting my feet off the ground to make myself go even faster. 'Good, good.'

'Find anything particularly . . . difficult?' Her eyes flicked to Iyabo.

Before the word 'no' leapt out of my mouth, I considered how to answer. 'Well, yeah. The self-defence.'

'Amber put in one hundred per cent effort,' Iyabo said firmly, putting her hand on my shoulder, which stopped me from spinning. 'She'll get there.'

I smiled at Iyabo, grateful that she stood up for me. For all her serenity, her nature was fierce too. She made me feel I could do anything. I guessed that's why she was here.

'Well dear, no one expects you to be an expert immediately.' Clara leaned past me and tapped away on the laptop.

Iyabo said, 'Clara's taking over now. I'll catch you later, Amber.'

For a few minutes after Iyabo had left, Clara didn't once glance up from her keyboard. I resisted the urge to talk for as long as I could, but I had too many questions.

'Clara, why am I here?' I blurted out. 'If you already observed me during the Escape Zone game, and the VR, what's this weekend all about? And, am I the only one here training?'

She smiled briefly but carried on typing without looking up. 'All in good time. Patience is a virtue, dear.'

It really wasn't! I'd spent over an hour being poked and prodded, then tossed to the ground by a (very nice) ninja. I deserved *some* answers.

'Clara, you *say* be patient, but if I had more information, maybe I'd know what to expect?' I remembered what Iyabo had said earlier. 'Don't *you* like to be prepared?'

Clara fixed me with a cool, steely gaze. 'And what if one *can't* prepare, hmm? What then? Thinking on your feet is essential. In this role, targets use the element of surprise to test you. You need to remain calm, assess your surroundings and keep your wits about you. Sometimes, really, that's all one *can* do.'

'Riiight. But, could you tell me if I need to watch out for booby traps? I'm not sure how many surprises I can handle.'

Clara looked up again, finally giving me her full attention. 'No, no booby traps. And yes, you're here training alone this weekend. Now, our final testing phase. Surveillance.'

'OK.' I wiggled, getting comfortable. 'And what do these involve?'

'Surveillance checks your observation skills and your ability to recall detail. You'll watch a short clip and answer questions.'

Clara spun the laptop around and pressed play. There was security camera footage on-screen, with people walking down a busy street, past a pub, with lots of cars and road signs. I stared at the screen, while Clara watched me.

Nothing much happened. The clip lasted about

twenty seconds. I kept on staring, letting my eyes flick over the screen, trying to capture everything I could. I think I did alright; it reminded me of memory card games I used to play when I was younger. Then I had to listen to an audio clip too and write down my answers.

Clara switched off the laptop. 'Right. I'll assess the results in my office while Iyabo comes in for the next test. I shan't be too long.'

As soon as she'd left, I spun round in my chair.

Within moments, Iyabo came back in. 'How did that go?' she asked.

'Who knows?' I sighed. 'OK, I think, but . . .'

She nodded. 'I imagine you're feeling drained. You're doing fine. The last test, you'll be glad to hear, is the polygraph, so it's helpful if you're not quite on top of your game, anyway.'

'The polygraph? That's the lie detector machine, right?' Excitement bubbled in my belly.

'Uh-huh.' Iyabo smiled. 'And afterwards, we'll break for some food.'

Thank God. I was starving.

'Right. IrisIdentify takes about fifteen minutes.' Iyabo sat down where Clara had, and turned the laptop back on. 'You've probably seen in films where a machine scratches lines onto a graph? Well, this one is a little different.'

'To be a good spy, I'd need to beat the machine, wouldn't I?' Asking Iyabo tricky questions wasn't as nerve-wracking as asking Clara. Iyabo was more straightforward.

'That's right.'

I nibbled my lip. 'I'm not a great liar though; it kind of makes me anxious.'

Iyabo chuckled. 'That's nice to hear.'

'So how do I become a good liar?'

Iyabo looked thoughtful before smiling gently. 'Try to notice if you blink during the test questions. Clara will ask a bunch as the 'base test'. There might be unexpected questions in there, so try not to be surprised.'

When Clara walked back in ten minutes later, she looked ecstatic. 'You've done even better than we hoped. There *are* areas to improve in, but that's only to be expected. Your ability to remember details in the surveillance exercise was top notch, as was your ability to pick out essential information during the audio.'

She clapped her hands together. 'Onto the poly. We'll do the base test first, so we can distinguish lies from truths. Amber, please rest your chin on this stand and keep steady. Look into the camera.'

Swivelling my chair around, I rested my chin in the groove that extended from the side of the laptop. Clara sat to one side of me and operated the laptop while I stared straight ahead; it was like being at the opticians, when they blow a puff of air into your eye.

Already I felt my heart rate speed up, so I focused on something happy—a memory of swimming in the sea with Vi when we'd been camping with her family. It worked, my mind cleared, and a relaxed feeling settled over me.

'Amber Roberts, are you fourteen years old?'

'Yes.'

So far, no problem.

'Do you have any brothers or sisters?'

'No.' I tried to keep my head still and my mind blank. *I'd have a brother or sister soon, right?*

'Are you worried about becoming a spy?'

'No?' I clenched my fists either side of me . . . Had my reply sounded more like a question? Was I getting this wrong?

'Do you have a boyfriend?'

'*Wha—!*' My chin jerked up from the panel and my heart galloped. 'Um, no, I don't!' I could feel my armpits prickling with sweat.

Iyabo snorted with laughter, but Clara didn't flinch, even though I'd practically shrieked.

'That will do.' Clara tapped away on the keyboard. 'I'll check the results before we continue.'

'Can I speak?' I whispered, turning my head slightly.

'Of course,' she replied.

'How does this test work?'

'I'm glad you asked,' said Clara. 'Your curiosity will stand you in good stead. The machine is designed to measure tiny physiological changes in the eye that occur when we lie. The pupil may dilate, or your reaction time might be delayed. How often you blink can also indicate the probability of lies.'

'Although lie detector tests have their uses, they are limited,' Iyabo added. 'I've got a book you can borrow on body language—it can often be a useful indicator.'

'But how can anyone beat the test?' I felt a surge of frustration. I wasn't any good at the martial arts and I'd be no good at this either! 'I can't control my body!'

'Did you ever do one of those staring contests with your friends?' Iyabo asked.

'The trying not to blink thing?'

'Mmm. If you find you *do* need to lie, the trick

is to be relaxed. Mix up the lies with the truth. Daydream, imagine a different response just before you answer, or bite down on your tongue. Those methods can work.'

'Now that we have a baseline,' Clara said, 'let's see if you can lie *intentionally*. Ready? Bear in mind Iyabo's advice.'

I rested my chin on the stand again, wondering if this was going to be any easier.

'Have you ever lied to your parents?'

'Yes,' I squeaked. I wanted to add, *only about The Agency*, but didn't. I cleared my throat, trying to keep my voice steady.

'Do you like Chinese food?'

'Yes.'

'Are you scared of spiders?'

'No.'

'Have you got any secrets?'

'No.' I scrunched up my fists, thinking of the Baby.

'We're finished.' Clara angled the laptop closer and tapped the keyboard.

I was relieved it was over. It felt intense being under the spotlight like that. Even when I was telling the truth I somehow felt guilty.

Clara asked, 'You like Chinese food?'

'No. That was a lie.' I smirked. 'Did I fool you?'

'Oh.' She frowned, her eyebrows coming together. 'Yes, you did. Well, let me order you a thin-crust pizza with pepperoni, extra chilli, but no mushrooms. Sushi for me. I trust that meets with your approval?'

My mouth fell open. 'How did you know that's my favourite?'

She blinked. 'Dear girl, your love of pizza is in every other HappySnap post!'

'Oh. Right.' The fact that she'd been stalking my posts was still unsettling, but I was starving, and the prospect of pizza was the best thing I'd heard all day.

Clara briefly tapped something on her phone. 'Alexei will kindly bring us our food, along with lemonade for you, Amber.' She turned to Iyabo. 'Care to join us?'

Iyabo shook her head. 'Thanks, but I need to make some calls. Great to have you on board, Amber, I'll see you first thing for some Krav Maga.'

'Thanks, Iyabo.' I was disappointed not to spend more time with her today. Clara was OK, but she definitely had a teacher-vibe. Iyabo already felt like a friend, as well as a mentor.

Swallowing the last mouthful of my pizza I was

suddenly overcome with tiredness. The thought of my king-sized bed and maybe a film or music was bliss, though proper spies probably didn't crash out after a hard day—I bet they had better stamina, and maybe even reports to write up or debriefs to attend.

I watched Clara pop the last salmon roll in her mouth, looking more like a posh magazine editor than a spy chief.

'Is it strange, having your headquarters underground and cut off from everything?' I asked.

She dabbed at her lips with a napkin. 'It's all I've ever known, dear. I was born down here. Both my parents were spies, though sadly they were killed on missions. You could say spying is in my blood.'

'Oh, Clara.' My eyes widened. 'Is that true?'

She waited a beat before answering.

'No.' Clara's face was deadpan before she smiled, revealing her perfect teeth. 'That was a fabrication. Did you not notice how I answered you so quickly? I gave you far too much information. There was also a lack of intonation in my voice and my body language remained static, even though I was talking about something as emotive and intimate as family. Clear signals.'

I blushed. 'Right.' Everything was a test with Clara. 'Listen and observe the details.'

'You've got it.' She patted my hand. 'Every interaction is an opportunity to observe and to learn. Always. You need to ensure you can detect lies, as well as tell them, dear.'

CHAPTER 10

Iyabo woke me up early for more martial arts practice and, although I ached like crazy, already I felt myself improving on what I'd learnt the day before. Then I watched an hour-long instructional video followed by a test about how to lose someone in a crowd, how to follow (tail) someone and how to change appearance quickly (always carry hair dye, make-up, hats, and sunglasses). I thought back to the VR experience, which I thought I'd messed up, but I'd actually used some of those techniques then.

Clara told me I was a natural, but that I needed more finesse.

'Your guard must always be up, Amber, and your attention to detail impeccable,' she said. 'Even when you think you can relax, you can't, not for a minute. You need to always remain one step ahead.'

So, although she thought I was good at this, I still had lots to learn.

As I packed my bag, my mind was buzzing. In a few hours I'd be back to my ordinary life—Mum, Dad, and the unborn bump. To Vi . . . I swallowed. Part of me wanted to keep this weekend to myself, to let it sink in, but it would look odd if I didn't message Vi as soon as I got home. She'd want to tell me about Tom's party. I'd need to say my weekend was dull so that she didn't get jealous or feel left out.

Clara and I emerged into bright Sunday sunshine. My eyes gradually adjusted after being underground with only dim artificial lights. She whipped on a pair of shades that I hadn't noticed her holding.

The car and Alexei were waiting. I put my bag in the boot then jumped in the back and lowered my window, ready to say goodbye, but Clara climbed in next to me! I wasn't expecting that.

She pulled her seatbelt across and peered over her sunglasses at me. 'We're very pleased with the effort you've made this weekend, Amber. Nice work.'

I smiled, reassured. 'Thank you.'

As we sped away, Clara took out a laptop. 'Iyabo in particular was most impressed by your can-do attitude. In fact, last night, I spoke to my superiors—'

Clara had superiors? I'd totally imagined she was at the top of this spy food-chain.

'—and they agree with me. You're ready to try your first mission.'

Nerves and excitement gurgled through me. 'Really?' I squeaked, barely able to stop myself bouncing up and down.

Clara nodded, with a closed-lipped smile.

'Um, but . . . how can that be right?' The excitement was already fading. *No way was I ready!* 'Don't I need more training?'

Clara glanced up from her laptop. 'And what do you think that training might be, dear?'

'I don't know.' I shrugged, thinking. 'Don't I need invisible ink and gadgets?'

Clara laughed, covering her mouth. 'The most effective way to acquire a new skill is simply by diving in head—or feet—first. If you wish to learn how to paint, picking up a brush is the only way forward.' She resumed her tapping. 'We'll meet during the week to discuss your assignment in more detail.'

I nodded. I had to trust Clara. I mean, I'd been warned about trusting *anyone*, but I guessed she was an exception, seeing as she was my boss.

I sat back and watched the countryside zoom

past, aware of her beside me, and then suddenly I realized this drive might also be a test. What had she told me? *Always be prepared.*

I sat up straighter and focused my gaze outside, committing to memory what landmarks and road signs we passed. I noticed fields with horses, a wind-power turbine and the electricity masts standing to attention. I checked my watch and timed how long it took us to get home. Turned around in my seat to see if any cars were following us.

As we got closer to my town, I allowed myself to loosen up. I opened the window a little and felt the refreshing breeze on my face while Clara tapped away on her laptop, and Alexei kept his eyes straight ahead.

When we pulled up outside my house, I didn't feel worried like last time. Now, my cover story was in place and Clara was with me too. She leaned forward and tapped the glass partition which lowered half an inch.

'I shan't be too long, Alexei,' she said, opening her door and stepping out. She dipped her head back in and said briskly, 'Come along!'

I stared at her open-mouthed as I climbed out of the car.

'Er . . . what's going on?' I asked, watching Clara

stride towards my front gate.

She rested her hand on the gatepost. 'I'm here to meet your parents, Amber. I've already spoken to your mother three times. She's terribly keen to hear how you've been getting along.'

My mouth dropped open, but no words came out.

'*But—*'

'It wouldn't be terribly responsible if your parents let you gad about with strangers now, would it?' Clara smiled. 'And it's useful profile-building for me.'

Right. I understood: she wanted to see what Mum and Dad were like, and their dynamic with me. It would be super awkward having Clara in my house, but there wasn't much I could do about it now. I grabbed my bags and followed her to the front door.

'Talk to Mum,' I whispered, as Clara's perfectly manicured fingernail hovered over the doorbell. 'She's the boss in our house.'

'Mothers generally are, I find,' Clara whispered back.

As we waited for the door to open, Clara added, 'Now, don't fret. I'll do the talking. Simply try to limit the . . . *animation* of your facial expressions. If you can.'

OK. That shouldn't be too hard. Ever since Mum's big baby announcement I'd distanced myself a little anyway.

Mum opened the door, holding out her arms immediately. She looked startled when she saw Clara and dropped her arms. I was a little disappointed. It had been a long, draining weekend and I wouldn't have minded a hug, but at the same time, I couldn't afford to be emotional . . . or *animated*.

'Oh!' Mum said enthusiastically, holding out her hand. 'You must be Clara.'

Clara? I bet Clara hadn't told Mum her real surname. *Spy 101, Amber!*

'Yes. We spoke over the phone. I'm Amber's tech mentor. How charming to finally meet you, Mrs Roberts.' Clara shook Mum's hand then took a 'business card' out of her Chanel handbag and handed it over. Mum barely glanced at it.

Oh, Mum. You'd make a terrible spy. Too trusting!

'Please, call me Ginny. Do come in. Excuse the mess.'

Mum always said 'Excuse the mess' to visitors, even though there never *was* any mess. She glanced at me.

'Your dad's at a car-boot sale, then he's stopping at the supermarket . . .' She trailed off and glanced sheepishly at Clara, as if embarrassed to be talking about ordinary stuff like this. 'Sorry that he isn't here to meet you.'

'Not a problem. I'm sure there'll be other opportunities.'

'Let's go into the kitchen.' Mum ushered Clara down the hall and I followed, feeling like I'd already been forgotten.

'I thought it would be useful to touch base, as it were,' Clara said briskly, sitting down.

Mum filled the kettle. 'Sounds great. Amber, do you want a drink, love? Clara, tea or coffee?'

'Coffee please. Black, no sugar, thank you.'

'Right.' Mum reached into the cupboard where she kept the matching cups and saucers, rarely used.

She was already impressed. Maybe it had been the Chanel handbag?

I poured myself a glass of apple juice and leaned against the counter, listening.

'As we discussed, the programme Amber's successfully become a part of involves ongoing mentoring. I'll be putting Amber through her paces with various STEM challenges and so forth.' Clara sounded persuasive and confident.

'Where and when will you be meeting?' Mum asked, filling the coffee pot.

'At Amber's school mainly, although there may be opportunities for being out in the community. Going forward, a further residential course is being planned, perhaps even European travel.'

Mum frowned slightly. Clara clocked it immediately, because she added casually, 'Only if she reaches a certain standard, naturally.'

'Naturally.' Mum plunged the coffee slowly and brought it to the table.

At the counter, I busied myself arranging biscuits onto a plate. Clara was so professional and composed; no wonder Mum bought every word.

European travel? I bit down on a smile. Now, where was my passport?

'As you can imagine, as Amber progresses academically, greater prospects will unfold. Travel and international contests will look impressive on her future university applications and CV, as you can appreciate.'

'Of course,' Mum said, pouring coffee into Clara's cup. 'I'm so delighted to hear that the government is subsidizing this. Let us know what we can do to support and encourage her, won't you?'

Please, Clara . . . don't dare say 'Extra homework'!

'There will be forms to complete, giving various permissions. But it's my job to keep you informed.

One thing I would bring to your attention is that we find candidates benefit from extra *physical* training, to balance out all the ... cerebral activity. Martial arts are excellent for mind and body. Enrolling Amber in a local class would be helpful. There's no need for extra homework, although learning additional languages is never a waste, if you'd like to consider that option. Young minds are so *plastic*, they soak up information like a sponge, don't you find?'

Plastic? A sponge? Ta very much.

I met Clara's eyes, and as she smiled over her coffee cup, I made myself focus on the smears her red lipstick had left behind.

CHAPTER 11

The next morning, as I was shoving my packed lunch into my backpack, my phone buzzed. Finally! I'd messaged Vi last night but hadn't received a reply.

Got dentist. Don't wait.

Hmm.

OK. See you for lunch?

Can't. Got detention.

What? That was a surprise.

Detention? What for?

Forgot my P.E. kit. Third time!

Bummer.

I stared at the phone and shouldered my bag. No reply. I headed downstairs, put my coat on and glanced at my phone again. I typed:

How was Tom's party?

No reply. Oh no. Was she . . . blanking me?

I'd been exhausted last night and after Clara left, I fell asleep. I never got around to texting Vi about my weekend. Was she sulking?

Walking into school on my own was lonely. I kept checking my phone, but she didn't reply. I hoped she wasn't too upset with me. Having fun during the Escape Zone game last week felt like a billion years ago. Now, I couldn't remember the last time we'd laughed together.

When I reached the school gates, I fired off one more text before I had to turn my phone off.

Hope dentist isn't painful. Fancy a rando cinema trip tomorrow night? We've got that EZ voucher, remember? Feels like I haven't seen you for ages! Miss you!

As Mr Andrews droned on about integers, I slumped in my chair. Double maths first thing was *not* my idea of a comforting Monday. *Ugh.* Understandably, I'd not taken any homework to the training weekend, so part of the reason I was so tired was because of staying up late trying to catch up.

It was true, what I'd texted Vi. I *did* miss her. I desperately wanted to be as close as we usually were, but it felt like we'd drifted, and I had no idea how to close the gap. Also, I wanted to talk to her about stuff. Obviously, I couldn't mention the spy training, but maybe it was time to open up about Mum. If I told Vi, she'd reassure me. Although I wasn't convinced that she'd understand how strange this was for me. She complained about her brothers often, but totally adored them.

When I got home yesterday, I noticed that Mum had started crossing off dates on the family wall calendar and adding Baby info. Only six months until the Baby arrived and then three would become four. The more I thought about the fourteen-year age gap, the weirder I felt. How would we ever get close or get along? By the time they were my age I'd be practically old!

'Wake up!' Mr Andrews' nasal tones sliced through the muggy school air. 'Amber!'

Oh no. Please don't ask me . . . His eyes burned through me like lasers. *Too late.*

'Um, forty?'

Mr Andrews glowered. 'Did you even *hear* the question?'

There was no point lying. 'No sir, sorry.'

'In your lunch break, perhaps you should examine exercise ten in more detail, hmm?'

Giggles started up behind me. I knew it was Taylor without even turning around because her laugh sounded like a hiccupping donkey.

'Ooh, Giraffe-girl got a lunchtime detention!' she hissed.

The back of my neck prickled. *Grr!* Had Vi actually spent all weekend with this . . . excuse for a person?

Mr Andrews walked to the back of the class and I felt my chair legs being kicked. I whirled around to find Taylor simpering at me.

'Lost your best friend?' she sneered. 'Saw you walking in all on your own . . . sad.' She put her fists into her eyes and mimed blubbing.

I held her gaze. 'She's at the dentist. Oh, didn't you know?'

Taylor didn't even blink. 'Her little brother is such a great kid.' Her tone sliced through the air. 'The party was *such* a laugh.'

I turned back around and focused on the questions on the whiteboard, my breath coming fast. I had to blink to stop the tears.

I didn't see Vi around school for the rest of the day.

As I was walking home, Clara texted and asked me to meet her in a quiet café on the outskirts of town, near the cinema. She'd attached the bus link. The route seemed straightforward, and at least I'd be unlikely to bump into anyone I knew.

I put my sunglasses on and pushed open the café door. I took in my surroundings: big squashy armchairs, watercolour prints and potted plants. I noticed Clara instantly.

'Would you like a drink?' she asked, sipping from a tiny cup.

'I'm OK, thanks.' I popped a piece of chewing gum into my mouth and glanced around as I sat down. A group of teens crowded around one glass of Coke, playing on a games console. Two old ladies shared a Victoria sponge and a pot of tea at the back. A businessman sprawled on a sofa with a laptop. No one was paying us any attention.

Clara leaned across the table and linked her fingers together. 'First,' she hissed, 'take those sunglasses off! We are *not* in a James Bond film for goodness' sake.'

'Don't you want me to look inconspicuous?'

'Amber! Wearing sunglasses indoors is hardly blending in. We wouldn't have recruited you unless you had the skills we need. It's precisely your natural ability *to* blend in which makes you a perfect *you-know-what.*'

She sipped her coffee.

A perfect spy.

'Your first assignment is—'

'A mission! Already?' I whispered, struggling to keep the enthusiasm out of my voice.

Clara dabbed at her lips with a paper napkin. 'I explained yesterday that we thought you were ready.'

'Right. OK.' I rubbed my hands together. 'What do I have to do?'

'Perhaps . . . not say "mission" for starters?' Although Clara's voice was stern, she was smiling, so I didn't feel too mortified.

'The job is to infiltrate an office space used by hackers. You'll go in and upload a virus which allows us to track precisely what they're doing on their computers by monitoring their keystrokes.'

I peered at her, not sure I'd heard correctly. 'You want me to do what?' I knew nothing about hacking and even less about computers. 'I'm no computer expert.'

'You don't need to be. We've emailed the brief to you. Encrypted, of course. It's fairly low risk.'

I didn't like the sound of that. 'Fairly?'

'We'll provide you with a disguise, laptop, and the external hard drive. We've arranged access and a pass into the building. No need to concern yourself about anything except uploading the virus into their systems.'

'When's this supposed to happen?'

'Tomorrow evening.'

'What?' I spluttered on my chewing gum. 'That's too soon. I'm not ready!'

'The less time you have to think about it, the better.'

'But I'd like to get, you know, *prepared.*'

'You don't need to prepare. Simply turn up, blend in, and upload. It's not rocket science.'

Maybe not for her!

'What are these hackers doing then?' I asked. 'Are they terrorists?' Hackers broke into computer systems and messed about or stole information, didn't they?

'As of yet we aren't sure. That's why we need to closely monitor them.'

'And where's the office? Will you send Alexei for me?'

'No car. It's only . . . see that office block across the street?' Clara nodded her head slightly. I turned to look out of the window to see a big office block on the corner.

Clara reached beneath the table for a slim black case. 'This laptop is yours to keep,' she said, putting the case on the table. 'You'll find your disguise inside too.'

I pushed the bag away from me slightly. 'I can't accept a laptop! I mean, I'd love to, but my parents might have something to say, you know?'

Clara rolled her eyes. 'Do stop worrying about minor details. I've already primed your parents and explained that it's a loan from the STEM programme to complete your assignments on.'

Of course.

'Read the assignment details and after you've completed the job, we'll meet for a debrief. I'll text.'

And with that, Clara stood, drained her cup and left.

Getting off the bus and walking home, I tried getting my head together. *Tomorrow?* My first mission was tomorrow? My mind reeled; I couldn't go home just yet. I took a slight detour and went to the park. Setting the case at my feet, I sat on an empty swing, replaying everything Clara had told me.

I could do this, couldn't I?

I checked my phone, no messages from Vi. Jeez. We'd never gone this long without contact before. This felt wrong. Someone had to reach out first.

I texted her. How was the dentist? Everything alright?

I couldn't tell her what I'd been up to, but I needed

to hear some friendly words.

Got set this horrible homework. Not sure if I can do it—feel underprepared!

I needed to know someone believed in me. I swung back and forth, dragging my heels through the overgrown grass. My phone buzzed and I glanced at the message.

You'll be fine. You've got skillz! Had a filling—agony! Cinema sounds good.

It was tomorrow night that I'd suggested for going to the cinema with Vi but now I was going to have to let her down. *Again.*

Unless . . . I could squeeze in both?

CHAPTER 12

In the same café as yesterday, in the loo, I was almost ready to start my mission. My phone rang and I grabbed it, fumbling, and nearly dropped it into the sink.

'Vi?'

'What time shall we meet then? I just need to wait for Mum to get back. The six thirty showing?'

I glanced at my watch, chewing my lip. I doubted that I'd be finished in an hour, although the cinema was near here.

'Sorry. Mum's got me doing a job for her. Reckon you can make the later showing?'

Silence on the other end. Then Vi gave a massive sigh, sounding irritated as heck.

'Seven?'

'Yes.' I felt terrible messing her around like this.

'The later one is showing on a bigger screen anyway.'

Silence.

'Or . . . we could try for another night if you want?'

'No. That should be alright. OK. See you outside just before seven then.'

All three toilets were unoccupied. *Good.* I checked my watch again. 5.50 p.m.—ten minutes until closing.

Dumping my backpack (with my change of clothes in to meet Vi after) next to the sink, I took out the black eyeliner Clara had insisted on. 'You need to look older, dear,' she'd said.

My black, bobbed wig made me look about three years older, at least. But apparently, I needed make-up, too. *Sigh.* I leaned towards the mirror and tried to pull my eyelid sideways with one hand, while using the other to drag the eyeliner along my upper lid, but the move was basically impossible; I was about to blind myself.

My stomach gurgled loudly. I should have eaten more at lunch, but I'd been too nervous.

I looked more *Distressed Baby Panda* than *Cool Goth Girl*, though my combats and hoodie were totally perfect for the part. I smudged the kohl pencil at the corners of my eyes. It'd have to do; this wasn't a fashion show.

Leaving the café, I headed across the road, my laptop bag swinging. Glimpsing my moody and mysterious reflection in a shop window, jitters sped through me, like I'd been force-fed popping candy.

I'd spent last night reading the mission brief. I knew enough about what hackers did to sound legit if anyone questioned me (which I *really* hoped they wouldn't).

My plan was to enter DropZone, a place where freelancers worked, access the Wi-Fi, and run the virus from a portable thumb drive. That would let The Agency know if DropZone was a genuine office workspace or a front for something more sinister.

Easy, right?

The Agency knew what they were doing.

And hopefully, in an hour's time, Vi and I would be munching salted popcorn and giggling like nothing between us had been strained lately. All the lying I'd done had made me feel rotten and I was determined to make it up to her, starting tonight.

Number 21 looked like any other office building. I pushed my way through a revolving glass door which opened onto a lobby, and instantly clocked the security camera mounted above me, on my left.

Good job my hood was up.

I tried ignoring my swooshing stomach.

Turnstiles. Escalators. Reception desk. Plants . . . hmm. Fake? Bugged?

I turned right so the camera couldn't linger on my face. A bald man sat behind the reception desk, flipping through a newspaper. Sweat trickled down my armpit.

Amber, chill!

Clara had explained that The Agency had built me a profile as a junior hacker, so that I could access the building. *I was allowed here.* I could act normal, like I came to this sort of place all the time.

Hide in plain sight.

Right? *Right.*

I sauntered to the desk. The security guard/ receptionist narrowed his eyes. For a second, paranoia prickled. Was he already on to me?

No, why would he be?

I concentrated on the signing-in book.

'Hey,' I croaked, making my voice two octaves lower than usual, as I scrawled an impossible-to-read signature in the book. 'DropZone?'

He half-grunted and motioned to the escalators behind the turnstiles. 'First floor.'

Taking my spy mobile out of my hoodie pocket,

I laid the QR code face down onto the turnstile scanner. A light flashed red before changing to green. I pushed against the metal bar to go through, but it didn't budge so I threw myself against it harder, and when the metal bar gave way, I nearly fell flat on my face. My cheeks flamed with embarrassment. I glanced around, but there was no one to notice what had just happened. Still, I needed to chill out. No shoving or pushing. I straightened my hoodie and waved a hand in front of my face to cool it down.

Keep your wig on, Amber. Style. It. Out. Use your brain.

My other, not-so-cool mobile vibrated in my back pocket. That'd be Vi, checking I'd left home already.

Not now, Vi.

Wiping clammy palms down my combats, I suddenly thought back to what I'd been taught at the training weekend. Maybe I shouldn't grab the escalator handrail, in case I left prints.

Well remembered.

At the top of the escalator was a long corridor with four doors leading off it. The first door, slightly open, was labelled 'DropZone'. I smoothed my wig, threw back my shoulders and walked in.

Fake it till you make it.

I'd expected a bright airy space full of creatives

and was surprised at how gloomy it was. I squinted. *No windows.* Thick cables bulged from bare concrete walls and extension cords trailed from floor-to-ceiling speakers playing tinny electro music.

Walking through the room, I almost collided with a massive stone pillar. I counted five guys and two girls spread out around large tables. Electrical wires and screens were everywhere. Conversation became quieter the deeper into the room I got. I could feel eyes on me—definitely *New Girl* territory.

A guy with wavy black hair, apart from one electric-blue streak at the front, leaned over a group, helping them work something out.

Act like you belong here.

My hand protectively on my laptop bag, I moved past him, towards a table at the back. He raised his chin in greeting and I smiled back, tight-lipped.

Please don't talk to me.

I sat at the table facing the door.

Always know your exits.

The thumb drive (a teeny black rectangle, smaller than my spy mobile) was in my hoodie pocket. I brought it out under the table and wedged it between my knees.

The conversation buzz increased. Thankfully, I'd been forgotten. Aware of whirring computers and droning fans, I unzipped my messenger bag, took out my laptop, dropped my spy mobile inside, and logged in using the Wi-Fi code I'd memorized. I opened a spreadsheet to cover my tracks and, certain that no one was looking in my direction, plugged in the thumb drive.

So far so good.

I exhaled in relief as the files started downloading (or was it uploading?), as Clara had assured me they would, once I logged in. I glanced around. The general 'look' was one that Vi would've described as *emo chic*: shaved or partially shaved heads, tattoos, and a few piercings. My combats and customized DMs fitted right in.

All I'd glimpsed on any of the computer screens so far were long strings of numbers. It hardly seemed like world domination, or whatever The Agency suspected these hackers were up to, but you never knew, right?

Expect the unexpected.

Gah! The progress bar was stuck! I wiggled the laptop back and forth.

Very technical, Amber.

I willed the computer to behave, glaring at the progress bar as it jerked and then slowly inched forward. I needed to work on my patience. Nothing

I could do would speed it up. The progress bar lurched and my phone, in my pocket, vibrated.

Stop messaging me, Vi. I'll be there.

I looked up and caught the blue-haired boy, stood over the far side, staring right at me. I flipped my head down. He hadn't been smiling, more like glaring.

The back of my neck prickled, but I forced myself to concentrate on the task at hand.

Come on, come on, come on . . . I regularly chanted this to myself during double maths—to deal with lessons that dragged on forever. Obviously, the stakes were higher now, but it made me feel better, like I was giving the computer a little pep talk.

Seventy-nine per cent.

'Alright?'

I stopped myself from leaping out of my seat. Bluey seemed to have teleported like a ghost to stand opposite me, arms folded. 'You're new.' He narrowed his eyes, giving me the once over.

A statement, not a question.

'Sure am,' I said casually, staring intently at my screen, as if I was working on an algebraic equation.

'Need help?' He tilted his head to one side, revealing a tiny skull earring.

Skulls weren't usually a good omen.

'I'm fine.' I shifted in my seat. *Say something friendlier.* 'Thanks though.'

'Some of us often grab a latte after a session,' he said. 'Join us and hang out, if you want. Always great to meet new . . . creatives.'

I started to shrug, before plastering a smile on my face. 'Thanks. Maybe.'

Now that I was looking straight at him, I realized his smile was fake, too—one of those smiles you give when you're not *really* feeling it. It didn't reach his dark, almost metallic, navy-blue eyes, which looked as dead as a shark's. I turned away and saw that everyone around us had their heads bent low, eyes fixed on their screens.

'What you workin' on?' he asked, brightly.

I flashed him what Mum called my 'winning smile' and tapped my nose. 'If I told you, I'd have to kill you.'

He grinned. He had dimples.

'Seriously.' He leaned over, hands flat on the table. 'Is it one of the . . . *big* projects?'

I glanced at his taut knuckles. One of them had a scar running along it.

A skull and a scar. Great.

'It's kind of big, yeah,' I said, turning back to my screen.

'And you're from I-Tech?' His smile was back to tight again and if I hadn't suspected before, now I was positive that Bluey was leading me into a trap (similar to when Taylor asked me to sniff her milk carton in Year 4. *Ewww*).

Nice try, Bluey.

'No. Logitech.' Miraculously, a company name from the signing-in book downstairs had leapt into my mind.

'Oh.' He looked thrown.

Good one, Amber.

'Look . . . Sorry, nice to chat, but I'm on a *really* strict deadline,' I said, watching the progress bar out of the corner of my eye.

Ninety-eight per cent.

I opened my messenger bag, preparing to scoop the laptop into it, when suddenly Bluey was far too close to me. So close I could feel minty breath on my cheek.

One hundred per cent.

I slammed the laptop shut and palmed the thumb drive, dragging it into my pocket, just as my phone buzzed again and Bluey jerked back, startled.

'Gotta take this!' I stood up quickly, shoving my vibrating phone in his face, but he was quick. Before I knew it, his hand was on top of my laptop.

I don't think so.

Surprising myself with my reaction, I seized my laptop and swung my bag around in one firm, impressive-if-I-do-say-so-myself move, then gasped as the strap and plastic buckle whipped Bluey across the face.

'Ow!' He put a hand to his cheek, wincing.

'Whoopsie,' I hissed, and then took off, flying down the escalator two steps at a time.

'Wait!' he shouted.

No chance.

I barrelled through the revolving doors just in time to see the security guard pick up his walkie-talkie. That wasn't about me, was it?

Had I blown it?

I sped down the street, my mind swinging like a pendulum. Footsteps slapped the pavement behind me.

Was I being followed?

Hearing a car screech to a stop, I dashed across the road. Hurtling along, I took a left down a side road back towards the main town square where the cinema was.

Thank God for athletics training! Tearing past the cinema, I smacked right into the back of . . . Vi! Her phone clattered to the pavement, and as she bent over to get it, I was already gone. If I'd stopped, she would've recognized me, and that could *not* happen.

Clearing the square, I heard panting behind me. A bus stopped and, skidding to a stop, I flung myself on.

My hand shook as I pressed my pass against the card reader. I moved down the aisle and collapsed into the back seat, gulping. I tore off my wig and stuffed it into my backpack. Then I turned around to look through the back window and saw a familiar flash of blue. The boy from the DropZone office.

GULP! And now he'd just seen me remove my wig. *What had I done?*

He waved something in the air, pointing to it with his other hand, smirking.

The bus moved away, and I turned to face the front. It didn't matter, did it? He didn't know who I was or anything. It'd be fine, right? I'd succeeded. I'd got the information that The Agency needed.

It was OK. My breathing slowed. I should text Vi, tell her I wasn't going to make it. Maybe I could say that Dad's car had broken down? More lies. I'd ask her to come over for a sleepover instead. Surely, she'd give me another chance? I was her best friend.

But . . . my phone wasn't in my back pocket. I rifled through the laptop bag—no phone, just the spy mobile. I hadn't taken my backpack off, so it wasn't in there—

Bluey had been grinning and waving something and he'd looked really pleased with himself.

He had my phone.

CHAPTER 13

Next morning, I woke up earlier than usual and turned on my laptop, scrolling through WhatsApp to read last night's horrible conversation between me and Vi. When I got in, I'd been buzzing from the drama of completing my first spy mission. Yeah, I'd potentially messed up at the end, and Bluey had my phone, but I'd got what I needed. I'd kept my cool for most of it, even though he'd freaked me out with his dangling skull earring and that scar on his knuckle.

I'd messaged Vi, who hadn't even tried keeping calm, but who'd let me have it.

Nice one for leaving me there like an idiot and ignoring my texts. All night.

I'm so, so sorry, Vi. I lost my phone!
Course you did.

Seriously—I spent ages looking for it.

Where did you last see it?

Somewhere in town. Dropped it running from the bus to meet you, I think.

You're lying. What's going on? Are you seeing someone?

What? No! Course not. You'd be the first to know if I was!

Really? Seems like you don't tell me anything these days.

I'd swallowed before replying.

You're my best friend, Vi. Always have been, always will be.

Things don't stay the same as when you're five, Ambs. Maybe we're outgrowing each other. I've seen more of Taylor and Layla lately. And they make an effort.

There's just some stuff going on at home right now. I'll sort my head out soon. I'm here for you. I am!

Actions speak louder than words, Ambs. You've been weird for ages. I reckon it's that STEM thing. You care more about school and impressing teachers these days rather than hanging out with me.

Vi, you've got it all wrong!

It was so tempting to tell her the truth.

What's going on at home then?

I couldn't be honest about that either. I wasn't ready to get into Mum's pregnancy because I hadn't got my head round it myself. Telling Vi, it made it even more real. I wouldn't be able to ignore it any longer. Didn't matter if I tried not to think about it. Of course, it was happening, wasn't it? I closed my eyes, feeling like a kid. A tear prickled the corner of my eye.

Mum's just a bit moody and stuff, I managed to type. Dunno. Sorry.

That's the only explanation I get? Right. Come back to me when you've got a real problem, alright?

'Offline' had popped up on Vi's profile. It was like a slap in the face.

And Vi didn't call round for me the next morning. This was THE WORST sign, it meant she was *really* mad. She'd only not called for me twice ever (once because I lost her new Sharpies, the second time because I spilled Ribena on her white jeans—both accidents).

I was late getting to school because part of me didn't want to leave the house in case I bumped into her, and then the other part of me kept hoping she'd forget our conversation and call round anyway.

I knew she was still *Moody Vi* the second I entered our form classroom. She wasn't a 'bottle-it-all-up' type of person—unlike me. But I wasn't going to avoid her either.

Vi glared at me when I slunk over and slid in next to her.

'Vi . . .'

My throat tightened—no room to squeeze out any breath.

'Again, I'm so sorry,' I jabbered. 'Because I had to get the bus, I got a bit lost when it got dark. And then . . . losing my phone . . . I'm *really* sorry.'

'Stop saying that!' she snapped. Her face was red, and the dirty look she gave me scorched through me.

I felt tears prickle in my eyes again. I dabbed at one that was making its way down my cheek.

'Amber . . .' Vi shut her eyes and let out a big sigh. 'Look, don't get upset. I just need to cool down, OK? You made me feel crap when you didn't turn up, and that was after we fixed the meeting time to suit *you*, remember? It feels like you're constantly messing me about these days.'

'I know. I don't mean to . . .'

'Then . . . maybe don't?' Vi's voice was frosty as

she opened her homework planner, but she gave me a little smile. I hadn't completely blown it with her. *Yet.*

My thoughts turned to my other life. Any pride in what I'd done right yesterday evaporated as I imagined meeting Clara for the debrief. What if those hackers were dangerous—Bluey now had my personal mobile. I wasn't even supposed to have taken it with me!

Had I put my family in any danger? Vi?

Was it even possible to juggle being a spy with a normal life? Some teenagers had acting and singing careers and school, didn't they? But then their lives didn't involve sneaking around and lying to the same extent. I'd failed Clara. She'd think I was useless and this whole spy thing would be over before it had properly started. If I couldn't keep track of my own mobile phone . . . why did I think I'd be a good spy?

I was rubbish!

At break Vi came over to me while I was sitting on a bench trying to revise for a chemistry test that I'd forgotten all about.

'Move over.' She sat down, bumping me with her hip, and took a banana out of her bag. 'So. What did your parents say about your phone?'

'I haven't told them yet,' I replied. 'Like I said, Mum was in a weird mood when I got in.'

Actually, that wasn't a lie. Dad had worked late and Mum had sent me to the chip shop because she was too worn out to cook. After we'd eaten, I'd gone straight up to my room because I didn't want to watch a programme with her about water births. *Eww.*

'How will you get another phone, though, unless you tell them?' Vi asked. 'Maybe it's insured? Have you called the bus station?'

'Not yet. I will though.'

'Don't worry,' Vi said. 'We've probably got an old one you can have. Maybe you could come over this weekend?'

I smiled at her. 'Yeah, I'd like that.'

'Good.' Vi peeled her banana and took a bite. I could tell that she believed me, which made me feel both better *and* worse about everything.

After school, I went across town again to meet Clara in the same café, opposite the office where I messed up my mission. What had I uploaded? What if I saw Bluey? He'd seen me take my wig off. Would he remember me?

I wondered if she was going to fire me on the

spot for being so clueless.

Approaching her table, I was more nervous than the time I got sent to the headmaster's office at primary school (I'd released the class butterflies, claiming no creature should be caged. *Save the butterflies!*).

'Amber. Please, sit down. I took the liberty of ordering you a double chocolate muffin and a lemonade. I hope that's acceptable?'

Totally acceptable, but if this was a *Good-Effort* muffin, she might want to take it back after discovering how I'd compromised The Agency. I pushed the plate to one side and sat down, sighing heavily. Better get it off my chest immediately.

'Um, Clara? The mission . . .'

'Yes, Amber.' She stirred her coffee and clinked the teaspoon against the side of the cup.

'It didn't . . . it didn't go as smoothly as you said.'

'How so?' Her smile was serene. She folded her hands over each other, a ruby ring glinting on her middle finger. She always looked impossible to ruffle although that might change any minute.

'A really nosy boy with blue hair kept hassling me, asking questions. I brushed him off and didn't pay much attention, but maybe I should have, because after I left, he followed me. I realized my phone—

not The Agency one—but my personal one, yes, I know I shouldn't have even had it, but . . . anyway, it was gone.' I closed my eyes and took a deep breath, before delivering the shocker. 'I'm pretty sure he—the blue-haired boy—has it. Well. I know he does.' I paused for breath.

She didn't answer, just looked at me with an impossible-to-read expression.

I picked at my fingernails and waited as Clara sipped delicately at her coffee, her little finger crooked as if she were royalty. Then she rummaged in a bag at her feet and brought something out.

'Here you go.'

My phone!

'I don't . . . Where did you get this?' I frowned, confused.

She smiled. 'Are you alright, dear?'

'Yeah.' I shook my head. 'But it's just . . .'

'Amber.' Her lips twitched in amusement. 'Last night was merely a test.'

I couldn't stop blinking; it felt like I'd been thrown down a rabbit hole, like Alice. *You what?*

'A test?'

'Yes. A *test*. We needed to understand how you'd fare in the field.'

I didn't know whether to be angry or thankful;

I was both. 'Right. So . . . you tricked me? Was everyone in on it?'

She nodded. 'DropZone is a real office space, but the blue-haired chap is one of ours.'

I slumped in my chair. Relieved but also . . . *annoyed*. I'd gone through so many emotions last night—I'd lost my phone and nearly ruined my closest friendship. All for some test? But then again . . . maybe it didn't matter so much that I'd messed up.

Every cloud has a silver lining.

That muffin was mine! I dragged the plate towards me, unpeeled the sticky wrapper and bit off a chunk, chocolate chips spilling onto the table.

'I didn't ruin anything then?' I asked, through a mouthful.

'Oh no, far from it,' Clara said. 'I'm sorry for the subterfuge. We wanted to place you in a real-life scenario to see if you're ready to operate alone.'

'And?'

'You did better than we expected, but errors *were* made. It's clear that, for a while at least, you'd be better off . . . working with someone.'

'*With* someone?' The roof of my mouth was clogged with chocolate and my words sounded thick.

'Yes, another recruit. We've the perfect babysitter

in mind.'

'A *babysitter*?' I was fourteen, old enough to *be* a babysitter, not need one!

Clara winced. 'Sorry. I mean teammate, colleague—what have you. We've an important mission that you'd both be perfect for.'

Excitement mixed with a sinking feeling in my stomach.

'Yeah?' I sipped my lemonade, then leaned forward.

Clara lowered her voice. 'A hacking group we've tracked for a while are becoming more dangerous. The general public have no knowledge of their antics yet, and we need to keep it that way. So far, they've managed to clear their tracks, but we're keeping a close eye.'

'What are they doing?' I paused, realizing this wasn't the best moment for blowing bubbles through my straw. 'Bringing down the western world?' I quipped.

Her expression told me to Be Serious. 'Well. Yes. They're attempting to do that very thing.'

My eyes widened. This wasn't a joke then.

'Their roots run deep. They've stolen information from government databases and taken significant amounts of money from financial institutions.'

'If it's such a big deal, why hasn't anyone heard about it?'

'Cybercrime often doesn't make the news, because computers and hacking are so specialized, and details are challenging to explain. But what they're up to is infinitely more serious than simply hacking social media accounts. The group has an international reach. Intel has located a specific group of teenagers operating out of an exclusive boarding school near Oslo.'

'How would I fit in?'

'We want you and the other operative to attend the school, undercover. We'll provide you with a different image and surname. The mission is to discover the group's aims and its mastermind. We've no idea if they're part of an organization called CHAOS, who we're already tracking, or something else entirely.'

'Don't you think a new girl turning up halfway through term will look suspicious?'

'That's why we set up the STEM programme, dear. The cover story is that you've been invited to the school for three weeks as part of an exclusive study group. Working on technology projects, like . . . a placement student. The school has twenty or more different nationalities, you'll fit right in.'

'Oh.' A muffin crumb lodged itself in the wrong food hole and I coughed violently.

'Here, dear,' Clara said, offering me my lemonade. 'Drink this.'

CHAPTER 14

At first, when Clara told Mum about the exclusive boarding school in the middle of the Norwegian countryside, she needed lots of convincing, but Dad researched the school thoroughly and was so eager for me to go that Mum finally came around.

I'd just finished packing.

'Come in!' I shouted, when Mum knocked on my door, keeping my voice light and bubbly.

I hadn't ever been away from my parents longer than three days before and although I was happy about the assignment, I was also nervous about heading into the unknown for three whole weeks. That was the same as half the summer holidays and they always seemed like ages.

Mum poked her head round the doorframe, and I beckoned her in.

Her voice broke a little as she asked, 'You've got everything?'

'Yeah, nearly done,' I said, wrapping my hairdryer plug around itself and zipping up my toiletry case.

'The opportunities falling into your lap right now are so wonderful,' she said, sitting on my bed and patting the space next to her. 'Sit with me.'

I sat down and she playfully nudged my knee. 'Are you worried about going away?'

I shook my head. 'Not really. I'm pretty excited.'

'Oh.' There was a long pause. I think Mum had expected me to need more reassurance.

'Well. *We're* going to find it strange, you being away. Who'll make sure that your dad doesn't overdo it on the snacking front?' She paused and then said, 'I also wanted to . . . have a quick word about the baby.'

Oh no. I didn't want to get into this right now. What if I said something I'd regret?

'I can tell this baby news is unsettling—'

Hmmm.

'I'm not clueless, love.' She smoothed her hands along the duvet cover. 'There must be a reason why you've barely asked me anything. Every time I mention it, you can't change the subject fast enough.'

Oh God! She was right though. I'd ignored any

mention of booties, baby names or prams—I either changed the subject or pretended I hadn't heard.

'If I'm honest, well, this might surprise you, but we're concerned how another child could . . . change our family, too. Nanna won't stop hassling me, now that I'm a geriatric mother, according to the midwives!'

Mum patted her stomach. 'But a new baby will just be . . . another one of life's delightful, unpredictable chapters. So, maybe, while you're away, you could take some time to consider the positives?'

I shrugged. 'Sure.'

Nope, Mum. That's the last thing I'll be thinking about.

She looked around at my posters on the walls and the bulging bookshelves, as if she needed to commit it all to memory.

'We're going to miss you so much.' She leaned over and kissed my cheek. 'Don't be much longer then, love. Clara texted to say the car's waiting.'

After she left, I sat there for a minute feeling bad. Then, I looked over the messages Vi and I had swapped earlier. The messages were friendlier than they'd been a few days ago, but still . . . we weren't quite back to our usual selves.

Ambs, can't believe you won't be around

every day. It's going to be boring!

I know. Don't forget about me, will you?

As if. Just make sure you're online every night.

Not allowed. Study school rules.

Seriously? OMG. Well, yeah . . . then I might forget who you are!

Hahaha. I'm serious. Don't have too much fun without me.

I'm gonna join that drama thing. You're not bothered, are you?

With Taylor?

God no. She hates that stuff, but Layla might join. They're alright.

You still planning on going to her party?

Yeah. It's on a dry ski slope thing. I've always wanted to do that.

Since when? You've changed!

Change happens to us all, or . . . should do.

I'll miss you.

You'll be too busy being the world's best nerd to think about me.

See you soon.

'Hi, Alexei,' I said cheerily, as he fussed in the boot

with the bags. I clambered in and wound down my window to wave at Mum and Dad on the doorstep, waiting to see me off. As we drove off, I swore Mum turned into Dad's shoulder . . . crying?

My throat tightened. Was Mum really going to miss me or was it just her hormones playing up again? I opened my eyes wide to stop myself crying, and turned to Clara, who was sitting next to me, reading a massive newspaper which took up half the back seat.

'Are you coming with me?' I asked.

'No, dear. I'm only here to ensure safe passage and to give you some items.'

'Like gadgets and stuff?'

Clara folded her newspaper and pursed her lips. 'We don't refer to The Agency equipment as that, but yes, I suppose there's no escaping . . . that's what they are.'

'X-ray specs? Invisible ink?'

Clara's nostrils flared.

'Listen carefully and be . . . *sensible*. We're dealing with advanced, expensive pieces of equipment. In many cases, only a handful have been created worldwide. Keep them on your person at all times. Be mindful that they aren't toys, despite their appearance.'

She rolled her eyes at my grin. 'I'm *serious*, Amber, and really, you ought to be too. If anyone outside of The Agency were to get hold of this tech, I'd hate to think what might happen.'

Clara shook her head and unzipped a case on the seat next to her. Out of it she took a round compact. She opened it and slid back the mirror to reveal a thin metal spike, like a prong.

'This mini tool will open any lock,' Clara said. 'Guaranteed access.'

No laser, voice changer, or grappling hook?

'What about electric doors?'

'No, but the school is a listed building, dear. This will come in useful, trust me.'

I pulled a 'meh' face though Clara was too busy rummaging in her bag to see it. 'What's next?'

Please let it be a mini TV-watch, or a shoe with a concealed dagger in the tip. Or at least poison darts?

Clara handed me a USB stick.

Wow. Exciting.

She caught my expression. 'You aren't expecting a *regular* USB stick, are you?'

'Oh.'

'This—' she waved it in my face—'is a recording device.'

OK. Pretty cool.

Then Clara's hand dived into the case for the third time. 'This is—'

'Nail polish,' I said, disappointed beyond belief. The colour was peach, not really my style.

She tapped the side of her nose, smiling. 'Not just *any* nail varnish.'

I managed to conceal a yawn.

'This is actually nitric acid. As you might recall from chemistry lessons, it is highly corrosive. If inhaled, it irritates and burns the lungs and throat.'

My heart sped up. 'You're joking?'

'I never joke, dear. This is only to be used in the most extreme circumstances, obviously.'

This *was* a big deal. I'd need to make sure I never let the bottle out of my sight.

'What about . . .' I couldn't believe I had to ask but needed to know. 'Do I get any . . . weapons?'

'Pepper spray perfume exists, though we're not giving you any because we aren't expecting much . . . violence, dear. If you find yourself in any unexpected or compromising positions, rely on speed and stamina. The basic moves Iyabo taught you ought to enable you to get away. Your colleague is fully combat trained, and an extraction plan *is* in place, if anything untoward should occur.'

Clara opened her own handbag. 'And we have

this,' she said, handing me a watch. Not any old watch, but the flashiest, most hideous pink thing ever, as if Barbie and a glitter-slime factory had co-designed a range of jewellery.

'I don't mean to be rude, or ungrateful, but this is . . . revolting!'

'I know!' She gave one of her rare, high-pitched laughs, verging on a giggle. 'Isn't it vile? But you need an object so ostentatious no one would dare steal it.'

'It's not for telling the time then?'

'Have you heard of an EMP device?'

I did my best impression of a goldfish.

'Electromagnetic pulses disrupt electrical devices. This watch acts in a similar way. When it's activated, by this little button, a short burst of electromagnetic disturbance is generated. Enough to affect any electronics nearby.'

'But I'd never wear something that flashy or bright . . . like, *ever*.'

Clara tutted. 'I appreciate that. And that's the point. But this assignment will only be successful if you adopt a new persona. It's irrelevant what the real Amber would or wouldn't wear, do, or say. Remember your training? You need to become . . . someone *else*. You're Amber De La Courte now. *Undercover*. Make sure you don't share any details of your real life with anyone at any time. It's too dangerous.'

The car turned into a deserted field.

'Where are we?'

'We're meeting a small private plane. We've had issues being followed—so this is an extra precaution. You'll be at Sankt Hallvard Manor in about five hours.'

Alexei turned off the engine. Clara and I got out, while Alexei lifted a large burgundy suitcase out of the boot.

'Are you going somewhere?' I pointed at her case.

Clara popped a humbug in her mouth and held the packet out to me. I shook my head.

'That's yours, dear,' she said, indicating the suitcase.

'It's not. My case is blue.'

Clara raised her eyebrows, her mouth puckered from sucking her sweet. 'First rule, dear. Know where your belongings are *at all times. This* suitcase is now yours. Your real case is in the car, too. Alexei has slipped it in the concealed compartment and will keep it safe until your return.'

But I'd taken ages choosing what to pack, everything I felt comfortable and cosy in. Who was I without my favourite clothes?

'I don't know about this,' I said firmly, irritated.

Clara cleared her throat. 'A new *identity* equals not only new skills, but new clothes too. How can you truly become someone else if you look the same? You've heard the aphorism "clothes maketh the man"? Well. Dressing in a certain way helps one act in a certain way. At least, I've always found that to be so.'

While we waited for the plane, I read over my 'personality' profile, and Clara told me about the targets I was to get close to and showed me their pictures.

When I asked about my 'babysitter', Clara said I'd be in safe hands with someone she trusted implicitly, who'd worked with them for years. I'd recognize the person, she said, and they'd already gone on ahead. It had to be Iyabo! That'd be brilliant. Having a temporary best friend while being away from Vi might make things less lonely. I hoped Vi wouldn't get too friendly with Taylor, who thought liking school and getting on with your parents was for losers.

Once the plane turned up, Clara stuck out her hand for me to shake.

'See you on the other side, Ms De La Courte.'

Sankt Hallvard Manor was *the* most impressive

building I'd ever seen. Surrounded by lush green lawns, it had the proportions of a cathedral, and once you'd walked through its entrance, everything inside was rich, dark wood and high ceilings. The doors had heavy iron knockers. It was as if I'd stepped into one of the costume dramas Mum liked to watch on Sundays.

She'd be having a cup of tea with Dad now, probably. Or eating. Along with pickled onions, Mum craved toasted cheese sandwiches with Worcester sauce, morning, noon, and night. I couldn't help smiling at the thought. I think she had two before I left this morning.

Then I remembered what she'd said, asking me to think more about the Baby. Even if I had the head space, what was there to think about? Nappies. No sleep forever. Having to hide away everything I didn't want to get trashed. Baby food splattered over the kitchen table . . .

Was there any chance that it could be . . . cute? Maybe? I could teach it some spy techniques, I guess . . . eventually, it'd get to an age where it could talk. Maybe I could earn extra pocket money by babysitting. Suddenly, I had a vision of my new brother or sister. Big eyes staring up at me. Maybe it wouldn't be *so* terrible?

I took a deep breath as I walked down a long corridor, following the signs to reception. I had no time to explore or unpack. My case had already been taken to my room and I was required to register immediately.

Now that I was here, I felt apprehensive. What if this mission went wrong? Did hackers go in for psychological or physical torture?

Stop catastrophizing, Amber!

I joined a long line in the main reception hall next to a banner that read 'Tech Placement Programme'. One entire wall was a giant computer screen, and around the perimeter were tables with laptops. I counted thirty people in front of me, all talking in different languages, all here to register for the tech programme. Hopefully I didn't stand out too much. I rearranged my little cross-body bag with my gadgets in. I'd left my spy mobile with Clara.

No going back now!

I felt eyes burning into my back. 'Placement students' was whispered, not quietly, either. I guessed some regular students were busy checking everyone out. My targets could be among the crowd, I realized, and a tingle shot through me. This was *real*. I was here, undercover, on a proper mission!

Clara had explained that the tech programme was

genuine; teens from a variety of schools across Europe were given this opportunity every year. I'd been briefed that the placement students would assume I was there on the same programme, so not to worry.

'Velkommen!'

I must have looked blank.

'Hello there,' the older man said in perfect English, smiling as I reached the front of the registration queue. 'And you are?'

'Amber—' I checked myself. 'Amber De La Courte.' I added a girly giggle to match my disgusting pink watch and he gave me an odd look.

Yeah, I know. Not really me is it?

I subtly concealed the watch under my jacket sleeve (I'd be hiding it as much as possible unless any of the targets were Barbie fans).

'OK, Miss De La Courte.' He withdrew a thick plastic card from a Rolodex and handed it over, along with a see-through lanyard holder. 'This is your campus ID and—' He reached under the table and everything inside me tensed, but he only brought out a branded cloth tote bag. 'Welcome to Sankt Hallvard Manor!'

'Thanks,' I said, my heart racing. I stepped out of line and peered inside the goody bag: notebook, pens, a branded hoodie, a baseball cap, and leaflets.

I put the ID inside the lanyard and placed it round my neck, sizing up the others waiting in line. Laughing and joking came from up front; three girls highly amused by someone or something. Not me, I hoped.

'Hi,' I said to them weakly, but no one heard me.

The source of their entertainment became obvious. A boy with wavy shoulder-length hair was doing robotic dance moves. When he span around, I felt a jolt of recognition. It was as if an ice cube had been put down my top. The last time I'd seen this boy was when he was waving my phone at me behind the bus, grinning smugly.

Bluey?

He didn't have a blue streak, but it was him alright. I was just backing off when he caught my eye and winked, quite obviously actually, which made everyone turn to stare at me.

'Amber! Hey!' He held up his hand for a high five, and I had no choice but to step forward and slap his palm hard enough to sting.

He knew my name. *This show-off was my babysitter!* I managed to keep the disappointment and horror off my face—I'd really been looking forward to seeing Iyabo.

The way the crowd were hanging off his every

word was annoying. I hadn't forgotten that arrogant, tight smile of his. He thought he was way cleverer than me, that was obvious.

We'll see about that.

I hated over-confident types. And I wasn't sure how subtle being a limelight-hogger was for a spy. At the hack place, he'd been grungy, and it had sort of suited him, but now he was more preppy, in a pale blue shirt with a collar, beige trousers and a—

Amber! Who cares? Get a grip, girl.

Feeling nervous and telling myself I was Amber De La Courte now, not Amber Roberts, I hovered nearby, aware of the stares aimed at the placement students by the others lining the back of the hall.

Bluey moved closer to me, and I noticed jealous glances from the girls who'd been lapping up his every word. *Yuck.*

'Feeling OK?' He swooped in and air-kissed me on both cheeks. 'We'll have to catch up in a bit.'

'What the heck are you doing?' I hissed through gritted teeth, combined with the biggest smile I could muster, which, FYI, is super tricky to pull off.

'Play the game, Amber,' he said through the noise of chatter around us. 'We're on the same side?'

Just then, the man registering everyone held his arm up and shouted: 'Quiet down, people! Surnames

A-K step to the left-hand side of the hall please, and L-Z move to the right. The prefects will escort you to your rooms.'

'Later, alligator.' Giving me another wink, he started to move away.

'Wait.' I grabbed his sleeve. 'Who are you? What's your name?'

He frowned, turning back. 'Luca,' he said, glancing around us with an odd expression. 'I'm Luca. We're at high school together, Amber . . . remember?'

'I'm—'

But in a flash, he'd disappeared, swallowed up into the moving crowd.

CHAPTER 15

'Here you are,' the prefect announced after we'd climbed a few flights of stairs and finally reached a door at the end of a long corridor. 'This is your room key. You're sharing with Beatrice Miller-Smythe. The dining hall opens in an hour.' He turned on his heel and left.

Sharing a room? Not what I'd expected. Should I . . . knock? This was my room too, but before I could decide, the door flew open.

'Are you coming in then?' a confident voice barked.

The girl leaning against the doorway had honey-streaked brown hair down to her bottom. She was pretty and—*oops*—unsmiling, looking infuriated in fact. Not a great start, especially since I recognized her: *one of my targets.* I wondered what strings The

Agency had pulled here.

I walked through the door, relieved to see my suitcase.

'Hi.' I gave her my best nice-girl smile. 'I'm Amber.'

'Uh-huh.' She gave a flicker of a smile before glancing at her nails. 'Beatrice.'

Real friendly.

I looked at the two wardrobes and the wooden desk positioned under a large bay window. 'This is a nice big room,' I said, determined not to be intimidated, walking over to the window and noticing that the room looked out onto a back courtyard.

Beatrice looked at me coolly from head to toe and then back up again. 'It is when there's only one person in it.'

Yowch!

'Listen . . .' She stepped away from the door. 'A quick rule to start. There's only one teeny bathroom, and I shower at night. Make sure you aren't using the bathroom between 9 and 10 p.m., and we'll get along marvellously, alright?'

Yes, my lady.

'OK. Sure. No problem,' I said, channelling my best clenched smile.

She looked surprised. Maybe she expected me to melt into a puddle in the face of her bossiness? Maybe she was being unwelcoming because she didn't want to share? Maybe placement students invading her school wound her up? Her body language was defensive and territorial: crossed arms and hands on hips.

Under Beatrice's snooty gaze, I heaved my suitcase onto the bed, unzipping it with my back to her. I didn't trust my facial expressions, considering I had no idea what Clara had packed. Remembering the school brochure, I turned and said enthusiastically, 'It's cool being invited here. Sankt Hallvard Manor has the most advanced technology lab and the best tutors in the country.'

'I know.' Beatrice moved to her bed and lay back on it gracefully, stifling a yawn. Of course.

Whatever.

'So . . . What's your favourite subject?' I tried again. Clara had given me background information—Beatrice's father owned a multi-million start-up company and her mother was a fashion designer—but I had to pretend I knew nothing, obviously.

'I excel at engineering and coding. Can't say I've a particular specialism yet.'

Modest much?

At my school, although I mainly hung out with Vi, we never seemed to get bored of each other and had never needed anyone else, well . . . not until recently, when Taylor and Layla had started muscling in. But only having one friend meant I had no clue how to make friends with anyone else, particularly someone like Beatrice Miller-Smythe.

I'd need to meet new people and step out of my comfort zone. Maybe I could try on Taylor's attitude for size? She was Miss Popular: I could channel her breeziness, but without the snark.

What had Clara packed? Opening the top section, I looked at a neat pile. I held up the first item, surprised: a knee-length dress. I was more a slouchy trousers and T-shirt person. Thumbing through, I could see everything looked smart. Nothing branded and thankfully, nothing as hideous as the pink EMP watch, but it *was* all quite . . . girly. Floral dresses, jumpsuits, ballet pumps—Vi would have loved it.

Digging underneath the clothes, seeing the logo of a silver cross, I squawked. '*Oh!*'

'What?' Beatrice snapped.

'Oh, nothing . . . well, just . . . *these.*' I held up the newest trainers on the market; they were lighter than air. Mum and Dad couldn't afford them, so I hadn't asked, but I swooned inwardly every time the TV ad came on.

'Do you run?' Beatrice asked, wrinkling her pert nose.

'A little. It's a good break from the intensity of coding.' I turned back to my case and took out a fluffy white dressing gown and a toiletry bag. 'Where can I put these?'

'Bathroom.' Beatrice pointed across the room and rolled over onto her side, watching me. She called out, 'You're quite right about keeping fit. I cheerlead and dance in my spare time . . . which we don't get too much of, but I like to try.'

I hung up the dressing gown on the bathroom door hook. Spotting an overlooked price tag, I quickly yanked it off. 'What sort of dancing?'

Maybe talking about her hobbies would warm her up?

'Contemporary, mainly. I've danced since I was two.'

Two? I'd barely mastered walking by then. She was a *perfect princess* and by rights, the type of person to wear the horrible pink watch I'd been given.

'Oh, Amber.' Beatrice had on a fake smile. 'The bathroom cabinet is like . . . *so super tiny*, do you mind not using it?'

I sighed. 'Right. Sure.'

I was just wondering how I'd manage one night

with Beatrice, let alone three weeks, when there was a knock on the door of our room. I couldn't see who it was from the bathroom, but I could hear Beatrice simpering, and imagined her fluttering those long lashes.

'Amber, it's for you,' she cooed, as I stepped back into the room.

Luca.

Ahh, no wonder she suddenly sounded friendlier.

'Hey, Ambs.' To my horror Luca kind of lunged at me and hugged me. It was essential to act like this was completely normal, so I hugged him back. He was muscly and as his stubbly cheek grazed mine, it felt like being squeezed by some sort of hairy animal. Mind you, a very nice-smelling hairy animal.

To one side, I caught sight of Beatrice tapping on her phone, pretending not to watch us.

Luca grinned like the fool he was. 'Want to go for a walk?'

'Er . . . sure,' I said. 'Hang on.' I dashed over to my bed and flipped the lid of my suitcase shut.

'See you later,' I told Beatrice.

'Cute,' she mouthed at me, smirking, before I headed out.

I closed the door and whirled round. 'Are you crazy?' I hissed, dragging Luca by his sleeve down the corridor.

'Nice to meet you properly, too, Amber. So now you know who I am?'

'Actually, I don't,' I said. 'Except that it was you who stole my phone.'

'I didn't steal it, you left it behind,' he said, maddeningly. 'You should have been more careful.' He tapped his head. 'Details, Amber.'

I inhaled loudly. 'Sorry, Luca. Not to sound rude or anything but . . . why have you come to my room? Wouldn't it make more sense to stay away from each other in public?'

He wrinkled his nose, tipping his head to one side. 'Why?'

'We don't want people seeing us together, do we?'

'Hiding in plain sight, Amber.' His smile was super annoying. 'Surely you've learnt that much so far?'

He was *infuriating*. Standing there, with his arms folded and a stupid black curl tumbling over his forehead and an eyebrow quirked at me as if I were a toddler—who did he think he was?

He perched in an alcove at the top of the staircase. 'Some friendly advice: the key to a successful assignment is making sure you're *liked*.

Here, especially judging by your roomie, we need to access the *popular* crowd. Her group are our targets. When people *like* you, they'll open up and tell you anything.'

'I'm on it,' I said. 'But no one likes someone who tries too hard.'

He shrugged. 'Good point. It's a fine balance between friendly and . . . being needy or sucking up, I suppose.'

'You've certainly mastered the art of the suck-up,' I said. 'That group of girls earlier were all over you. I mean, each to their own. I guess some people like show-offs.'

He laughed, and I tried not to notice he had a nice smile, or those dimples. Instead I focused on how annoying he was.

'I like your hair, by the way, lots of natural lowlights in there,' he said. 'I mean, it's better than that wig.'

I flared my nostrils.

'Seriously. It's pretty.'

Was paying me compliments supposed to put me at ease? I stared at him, unable to ignore the fact that his eyes were startlingly blue. *Contacts?*

I sniffed, disdainfully. '*Your* hair looked better blue.'

'What can I say? I'm a chameleon.' He paused, then changed his tone from smarmy to serious. 'Look, we have to work together. We might as well try to get along. Let's start over. Anything you want to ask me?'

Why do you think you're so hot?

'How old are you?'

'Sixteen.'

'And how long have you been a—' I looked round, making sure we were out of earshot. 'A spy?'

'Four years.'

I gasped. 'Since you were twelve?!'

'Clara was right—you *are* good with numbers.'

I rolled my eyes.

He tapped my arm lightly. 'Seriously. You read the profile, right? Our cover is that we're from the same school. We're supposed to be in the same year and good at tech, so don't you think it'd look bizarre if we *didn't* speak?'

I felt my cheeks heat up because when I was on the plane I'd barely skimmed that section of the profile. My bad. I'd been too focused on reading about the targets.

'Yeah. Of course. I know that.'

'Anyway, I'm starving.' He stood up. 'Let's get some food and check things out. Just take my lead and enjoy getting into character. Don't worry, it'll be fine.'

Now, he *almost* sounded like a nice guy.

I was too tired to keep up the snarky act, so I followed him downstairs into a massive, noisy dining hall full of students. Three separate food stations—meat, vegetarian, and vegan—had screens above them listing food choices in different languages.

Luca and I headed for the meat counter and helped ourselves from the buffet selection. I chose chicken tikka kebabs with salad, and he loaded up a cheeseburger with *five* different toppings, including chillies.

'What?' he said, affronted by my expression. 'I'm a growing boy!'

Luca took his tray and marched towards the main area where tables were set out in long lines. He plonked himself in the middle of a crowded table with one space next to him.

That was where I'd be sitting then.

Was this his cover persona, or was he always so . . . confident? His attitude seemed risky. Surely there was more benefit in holding back, taking in your surroundings and assessing who was who?

As I sat down, I smiled shyly at the others at the table; they looked up from their conversations. I recognized two faces from the photos Clara had shown me. A boy with a blond buzz cut and even sharper cheekbones, and a pink-haired girl eating noodles.

Aha. So, Luca had chosen this table deliberately! He was already in full-on mission mode. I needed to get into the same zone. There was no harm following his lead for now—I mean, he clearly knew what he was doing. And there was no way I wanted him to think I was slacking, or not up to the job.

'I'm Luca and this is Amber,' he said, indicating me. 'We're a part of the three-week advanced placement programme. We're from Kiko High in the UK.'

'Never heard of it, but then that's not a surprise.' The boy with the buzz cut turned his mouth down, looking at the two girls at the table, who both shrugged. 'So many schools come through here.' He smiled at us. 'I'm Jay.'

The girl eating noodles with chopsticks tossed her pink-tinged fringe out of her eyes. 'Ruby,' she said. 'The tech programme is really competitive. Guess you're pretty smart?'

'Super smart,' Luca joked, making a very dopey face. They all laughed.

The other girl had a brown bob, pimply skin and held herself more stiffly than the others. I didn't recognize her from Clara's info. She twirled a strand of hair round her finger and said quietly, 'I'm Penny. What electives have you signed up for?'

'Er . . . not sure.' Had Clara mentioned my classes? Maybe I'd skimmed that section of the brief, too. *Gah!* What else had I missed? Stressing over me and Vi had scrambled my brain.

Luca playfully punched my shoulder. 'Oh, *Ambs*, sometimes you're *such* an airhead!'

Ambs? Airhead? Before I could kick him under the table, he reached over and grabbed my lanyard.

'We signed up to classes when we applied . . . remember? *Duh!* Check your ID card.' He jiggled it.

Uh-oh. He knew something I didn't. I flipped the ID card back and forth and, after tapping it, was startled to see it blink into life and transform into a mini tablet. While I scrolled through my class options, Luca accessed his.

'I'm signed up for computer science, digital literacy, coding, and track,' he said, smiling, dimples popping.

'Same as me,' the girl who'd asked said, staring at Luca before quickly looking down at her plate.

Was she blushing?

There were other murmurs and nods round the table.

'Oh, yeah, I remember now.' I rolled my eyes.

'Seems ages ago we booked, doesn't it?' I twisted my ID card around and recited my classes.

'HTML, robotics, track, and . . .' My heart pounded so loudly, I was surprised no one else heard it. 'Debate.'

'You'll be with me and Queen Bea.' Ruby sniggered.

I gulped. *Debate?*

'Track? Cool, me too.' Luca grinned, but I hardly noticed.

Debate was standing in front of people and speaking; proving your point by . . . arguing. I *hated* talking in big groups. I always let others do our school presentations. I didn't mind talking one-to-one but . . . what was Clara thinking?

Debate was my idea of absolute hell.

CHAPTER 16

I'd been at Sankt Hallvard Manor for three days and I'd done my best to kick into spy-mode. I'd used the little lock-picking set to bust into Bea's side drawers but hadn't found anything useful except lists of bank statements and a credit card application. I'd skimmed the figures which had seemed large for anyone, let alone a teenager, but hadn't found much in the way of information we could act on.

Luca, who had the talent of putting people at ease and gaining their confidence, already knew the hackers as intimately as their background info. He told me not to stress, that sometimes girls found it harder than boys to get into established groups, but that I should keep trying.

Annoying. But I was determined. I needed to become more comfortable with my persona and adopt the same rich-girl confidence of Beatrice and her friends. Though I was sure at least one of them was faking an attitude, too. Penny seemed more timid than the others. Watching her body language, she often looked ever so slightly sad or worried, maybe.

Lessons-wise, nothing had been too problematic so far. No one paid the placement students much attention; I took extensive notes and listened. In HTML and robotics we worked in small groups, and I'd not yet been placed with any of my targets, so didn't mind when others took the lead.

But now, the first dreaded debate class had come around. No way could I wriggle out of this one, even though I'd just wasted five minutes pretending I couldn't find the room. I told myself it would be good for me, even if I was quaking inside at the thought of standing up and speaking in front of a big group.

'Welcome to debate!' the teacher announced; she had a slight German accent. She strolled around the classroom, hands behind her back. She was smartly dressed and looked gentle, but her small brown eyes were sharp.

'I'm Professor Ellery. I'm aware our placement pupils may not have much experience of debating in a formal setting, so I'll explain how this works.'

Steepling her fingers, she positioned them

under her chin. 'Here at Sankt Hallvard Manor, we recognize that debating current topics is a guaranteed way to build confidence, articulate thought processes, convince others and think on your feet. Valuable—nay, essential—skills in the working world.

'The art of debate goes beyond mere discussion, however. *Formal* debating has two sides, with one *for* and one *against* the issue being debated. There are winners and losers and point scoring. We'll all be working towards The Big Debate in a couple of weeks' time. An annual event here at Sankt Hallvard. Now, as a warm up and introduction, I'm going to ask two of you to leap right in. I'll give you ten minutes to prepare.'

She weaved in and out of chairs and tables, looking at us keenly as we fumbled with our textbooks.

She stopped and placed a hand on my desk. *Oh great!* I rubbed my sweaty palms together. Leaning in, she said, 'Amber, is it? We'll ease you in gently. Ethics of animal testing, please. Take the position of . . . against.'

My face heated up as if I was too close to a fire.

Professor Ellery put her other hand on the table across the aisle. 'Ruby. You take the *for* position. Ten minutes to research, using the internet, and then both of you come to the front.'

Animal testing?

I opened the desk tablet and gazed at the screen. Then I jotted into a notebook: *It's cruel.*

Ruby was busy writing things down. I wondered if, because we sort of knew each other, she might go easy on me.

Ten minutes later, Ruby slid out of her seat, smoothed down her maxi dress and glided to the whiteboard. I very nearly tripped over my bag as I trotted behind.

The class wasn't huge, maybe fifteen teens, but instead of looking bored and distracted like in any regular classroom, everyone was concentrating on us.

Professor Ellery perched beside us on the edge of her desk. 'Amber, you may begin.'

I cleared my throat. *Here we go.*

'Right. OK. Well, the issue of animal testing is a controversial subject with . . . many issues to consider,' I began, thinking this was going fine. Then someone heckled me.

'Stalling!' Beatrice piped up at me from the front seat, while beaming at Ruby.

'And, furthermore . . .' I looked down at my notes. I'd scribbled them so quickly I could barely read my own writing.

The classroom buzz was growing and I caught Professor Ellery watching me intently, her eyes burning.

'*And furthermore* . . . experiments can cause pain to animals.'

Someone at the back snorted with laughter. 'You don't say!'

'Don't worry, Amber, you're doing fine.' Professor Ellery stepped in. 'Heckling is part and parcel of the debate scene.' She nodded at my paper. 'Try and ignore the comments and carry on. Then we'll hear from the opposition.'

Managing to hide my shaky nerves, I carried on for another two minutes—expanding on how the benefits of animal testing to humans hadn't been proved—but my weak arguments and delivery had lost me the audience's attention. Maybe I could never have won anyway? I just didn't have the same confidence that the others had, the kind of confidence that meant they could read out a shopping list and still get applause. I needed to fake it till I made it, especially because I didn't have the luxury of time.

Still, when I finished, instead of looking at the floor, wishing the ground would open, I made myself lift my chin and look out at the audience. I focused on staring at people's ears . . . Iyabo had told me that was a good way of *looking* like you were looking at people, without being distracted by their facial expressions.

When it was Ruby's turn, she spoke as if she was selling ice to snowmen who didn't even know they needed it. Her argument was strong and solid regarding humane ways to test products. It was only when she listed the source of her scientific breakthrough information that she faltered and froze mid-sentence. Seeing her panicked expression, I empathized. It was exactly how I'd felt inside, and I wouldn't wish that on anyone.

Maybe this was an opportunity to make friends?

I caught Ruby's eye, tipped my head, and mouthed 'Lancaster University study' at her, the only thing I'd remembered from my research, and she smiled gratefully at me.

Small victories.

Eventually, the bell sounded and everyone filed out. I needed to do *much* better. I'd need to study, not only debating topics, but how to project more confidence too. *Ugh. Epic fail.*

As I packed away my pencil case, a hand landed on my shoulder.

'Amber, I could tell you became a little scrambled up there.' Professor Ellery was beside me, smiling sympathetically. 'But I wanted to say well done. You kept a cool head despite the occasional hiccup. If you email me, I'll suggest some texts on debating techniques. A good trick to remember with debate is . . . you don't need to be correct. Often, especially in moral and ethical arguments, there is no "correct" answer, you simply need to sound convincing, as if you know what you are talking about.'

Basically, she thought I was rubbish. She might look like my nanna, but Professor Ellery obviously knew how to whip her students into shape.

Fake it till you make it.

'Thanks, Professor,' I said, forcing positivity into my voice. 'Good advice.'

'No problem.' Her brown eyes glinted at me. 'Just relax and you'll do fine.'

We'd see about that. In the meantime, I'd need to sharpen my acting skills. I suddenly missed Vi badly. She didn't hang around waiting for approval or doubting she was as good as anyone else. She just went for it. I needed to do the same.

I'd love to see her face right now.

A warm feeling washed over me; maybe I *could*? Clara had told me not to access social media, but using a library computer would be alright, surely? We'd been given a school log-in and email address so I couldn't see the issue . . . and anyway, this felt like an emergency.

The past few days I'd tried hard to make friends with people who I had nothing in common with, who didn't get me, who'd probably never understand why, exactly, baked beans are so disgusting. But back home I had a friend who hadn't deserted me, despite me repeatedly letting her down and acting like a weirdo recently. She was kind and forgiving and accepted me for who I was. Vi was my people.

Happier, I dusted myself off and headed to the library.

Sankt Hallvard Manor library was as stately and opulent as the rest of the place. The latest laptops, scanners, and printers sat on the desks, but the rest of the room was comfortingly old-fashioned. And best of all, with everyone at lunch, it was deserted.

I chose a table along the back wall so I could see who walked in, and keeping a lookout, I logged into Vi's HappySnap account—we knew each other's passwords, always had, in case of an emergency of the snooping-parental type.

Scrolling through her recent photos, I smiled: there was Monty, her cockapoo, and Vi messing around with her two younger brothers. She *was* bored! I really wanted to message her.

Oh.

Moving down, my finger froze. She wasn't bored. *At all.* There were heaps of photos with filters of . . . her and *Taylor*! A sinking feeling filled my stomach. Vi had promised she didn't even *like* Taylor!

They'd gone bowling. Photos of them outside the town hall posing under a poster for auditions had been captioned: 'Stars are Born!'

I don't know how long I stared at Vi's photos, but it felt like hours. She'd already replaced me? I genuinely wanted to burst into tears.

A movement in the library doorway jerked me out of my misery. I glanced up.

'Amber.' Professor Ellery was coming towards me, books under her arms. 'Swotting up on debate tactics?'

'Er, no.' I closed my laptop. 'Just doing some research for another project.'

She nodded, shifting the books under her arm, then cocked her head to one side.

'I sense you're feeling lost,' she said.

Yeah. That was *exactly* how I felt. Hearing it out loud nearly made me cry but something stopped me.

I was here to toughen up, not to give in to every wobbly feeling I had.

'I'm fine, Professor,' I said, smiling. 'I really am.

But thanks for asking. That's kind.'

'My pleasure, .' She nodded again. 'What school did you say you attend? I might know it . . .'

Um. K . . . something. Think. Think.

'K-k-kiko High,' I said, stammering a little.

Was she giving me a weird look? Did she know I was lying?

'I can't say I do know that school,' she said eventually, with a puzzled expression.

'Well, I must get on. Don't isolate yourself. Get out there and mingle!' She turned and walked over to a far table. I watched her open one of her books.

For about five minutes I googled 'perfecting debate skills' until I figured it wouldn't look suspicious if I left.

As I walked out of the library, I felt myself toughening up again. I just needed to grow a thicker skin. *OK.* So . . . the Sankt Hallvard Manor lot *were* a little stand-offish and intimidating, with many of them having more money than sense, but I remembered something Mum had told me once when I got nervous before a school test. She said to imagine teachers on the loo; everyone had the same bodily functions, even royalty, and I needed to remember that.

I could do this. I could get them to welcome me into their clique and find out their plans . . .

CHAPTER 17

I woke up with the sound of the door quietly closing. I opened my eyes and squinted against the steamy haze from the bathroom which had gathered around my bed.

Beatrice's nightly shower. *Of course.*

I blinked and looked over to her bed—empty.

'Bea?' I sat up and peered towards the bathroom again. 'Are you in there?'

Silence.

This wasn't the first time I'd woken up to find her AWOL. It had happened the night before last, too. I'd put it down to a sleepover in Ruby's room. One in Penny's was unlikely. She definitely wasn't as popular. I'd already noticed how Bea and Ruby subtly put her down.

Time to see where Beatrice was going. I got up

and changed into a pair of leggings and my hoodie. I slipped my recording USB stick into my pocket. I decided not to put my new trainers on, I'd be quieter without them squeaking on the floorboards.

I slipped some loose change into my hoodie pocket. *If anyone asks, I'm thirsty and in search of a vending machine*, I told myself. Cover story secured. I reckoned Clara would nod in approval at my thought process.

I tiptoed down the hall, putting my ear up against the doors I passed, listening out for any sounds of giggling, or Bea's voice. Nothing. At the end of the hall where the back stairs led down to the dining room, I paused. *A banging sound.*

I froze, trying to locate where the sound was coming from, but it stopped. Feeling tense, I was about to creep down the stairs when something touched my shoulder.

'Agggggh!' I jumped back, my heart nearly shooting through my mouth.

'Sleepwalking, Amber?'

Beatrice stood behind me, dressed in lycra leggings and a cashmere cardigan, with big fluffy booties on her feet. Her hair was still a little damp from her shower and curled around her face.

'I was on my way to the vending machine,' I told

her, trying not to sound as breathless as I felt. 'You?'

She smiled, mysteriously. 'I was about to go for a late-night workout,' she said.

I smiled and forced myself to meet her piercing gaze. 'Really?'

She tilted her head to one side. 'Oh, yes. I read an article about how midnight workouts are the best. They keep your heart rate elevated and you burn calories all night long.'

Ridiculous! 'Good for you.' I paused. 'Do you always shower before you work out?'

'Of course. Who wants sweat on sweat? Er, *gross.*' Bea didn't skip a beat. 'I changed my mind though,' she said. 'Too creepy in the gym at night.'

Something occurred to me and popped out before I could consider whether I should have said it. 'But don't you get to the gym by the stairs?' I gestured in front of me.

I'd have seen her come up. But she'd appeared *behind* me.

Beatrice laughed, which was kind of shocking because I didn't know if she was capable of actual laughter—all I'd heard from her until then was snorts and sniffs.

'Don't you know about the lift?' she said, leaning in closer. 'It's supposed to be staff-only, but it's a good way of getting around.' She gestured behind her.

'Oh, right.' I nodded again. 'Good tip, thanks. Well, I want a drink, so I'll see you later.' I padded down the stairs, not stopping till I reached the vending machine next to the cafeteria. As I waited for my bottled water to drop into the tray, I frowned at my reflection in the glass.

Beatrice's story was plausible. It wasn't that which had raised my suspicions but her unusual friendliness. *Total alarm bells.*

Something was going on. Next opportunity, I'd find out exactly what.

The next morning, Beatrice was back to her snappy, chilly self. Maybe I'd been too quick to suspect her of anything. If she really was up to something, wouldn't she try to be nice and put me off her scent? Obviously not.

I decided to speak to Luca over lunch. Two heads and all that.

The dining hall was quiet and there was no sign, or sound, of Luca.

Beatrice, Jay, and Ruby had their heads together, discussing something intense by the looks of it. Luca had told me that Elliot, his room-mate, was one to watch, but I hadn't had much contact with him yet.

Penny sat a few seats away from the others, reading. I couldn't see the book title, but when she shifted her arms, I noticed an image of a robot on the front cover.

I got myself quiche and salad and then sat opposite her. The others didn't even glance up. I was able to read the title of Penny's book now: *Asimov's Laws of Robotics Are Wrong*.

'And are they?' I asked, nodding towards the book.

She lowered it. 'Sorry?'

'Wrong?' I pointed at the cover. 'The laws?' I spoke slowly so that my voice didn't shake; I was nervous singling her out like this. I squeezed my toes hard enough to bring on a cramp.

Her small smile turned into an about-to-laugh-grin. 'Have you read Asimov?'

'No, but I liked the film *I, Robot*, isn't that him?'

Her whole face lit up. 'Sort of.'

As we ate our lunch, she explained more than I needed to know about the laws of robotics but managed to make it sound interesting; maybe I'd check out Asimov's short stories.

Why hadn't I done this sooner?

'Hey! Where's lover boy?' Beatrice's plummy tones rang out along the table.

'What?' I asked.

Jay leered. 'Don't you mean *who?*'

Recovery, Amber. Recovery.

I surprised myself by blushing at will and opening my eyes wide.

'Luca? I'm not sure . . .' I put a deliberate falter in my voice and pouted. 'I haven't seen him, but—' I smiled then added, 'He'd better show up soon. I need my daily shot of those baby blues.'

Everyone laughed.

'*Baby!*'

I spun round, horrified to see Luca grinning at me. 'I'm sorry I'm late.' He winked and blew me a kiss. 'Sweet bae!'

My cheeks flared red again, but this time it was involuntary. How embarrassing! I hoped Luca didn't think I meant what I'd just said.

Think in character, Amber. Better if everyone thinks you and Luca do have *a thing* going on . . . they'll be less likely to suspect anything.

I laughed along with everyone else, and caught Beatrice and Ruby looking at me as though they were seeing someone they now wanted to be friends with—all because I might have a boyfriend!

Probably best to continue the pretence for the rest of our time here.

Ugh. That would be annoying.

'Come and sit here.' I patted the seat next to me and Luca sat down with his piled-high plate: an omelette and a burger, along with chips. That boy sure could eat.

The attention drifted off us and when Beatrice and her gang had left, I leaned into Luca.

'That was an act, by the way,' I told him archly, my cheeks feeling warm. 'Just so you know.'

'And very impressive it was, too,' he said, chuckling and polishing off the last bit of omelette on his plate. 'Not to mention flattering.'

I opened my mouth, wanting to burn him with a witty comeback, but then I remembered what I really wanted to talk to him about.

'I think I've stumbled across a lead,' I said.

'Uh-huh.' His eyes twinkled; they were so blue and burned right through me.

'I think, though I can't be sure . . . that Beatrice does something at night. I mean, she disappears after her shower when she thinks I'm asleep. I caught her last night and she said she was going for a workout, but . . .' I paused, thinking. 'Her story adds up, just about—technically it's possible an insane person would consider working out at midnight . . . except there's something off about it.'

Luca dabbed his mouth with a napkin.

'Good work, you should keep an eye on her,' he said, then hesitated. 'And keep up the lovesick act. It's a good distraction and . . . highly amusing for me.'

I shook my head, rolling my eyes. 'Haha. Get over yourself, Luca,' I said, grabbing my bag and heading for my next class.

I strode to the door of the cafeteria and made the mistake of turning around when I got there.

Luca was staring at me, but for once the smug smile on his face had vanished.

CHAPTER 18

By the start of week two, moving outside my comfort zone was working better than I could have imagined. I was getting to know Penny better. She was a science and computing genius, and for the next few days, we often sat together at mealtimes; she'd tell me about her latest experiments and discoveries. She was at Sankt Hallvard Manor on an academic scholarship, which I guessed meant she wasn't as wealthy as the others. She'd come here last year, so was definitely on the outside a little.

Even though she hung around with the other four, her profile hadn't been in Clara's intel. Part of me hoped she wasn't involved with the hacking, because I liked her. Besides, I had nothing tangible to go on about anything. *Yet.* I'd heard no mention of hacking or anything that might be useful. As far as I could tell, they were normal teens talking about the usual: music, TV, money, schoolwork, and other people. Luca mumbled that Elliot liked Beatrice (in 'that' way), and that Jay might be gay. But between us that was the only new information we'd discovered that hadn't been in the brief. We'd failed to actually pin anything on anyone. The financial statements that I'd found in Bea's drawers hadn't contained anything recognizable.

From my observations and Luca's, I focused on profiling the group, in terms of pecking order.

- Beatrice. Most popular, but not the smartest.
- Elliot. Keeps himself to himself. Fancies Bea (according to Luca).
- Ruby. Hangs off Bea's every word. An airhead and a follower.
- Jay. Cute, but neutral, goes along with others, popular nerd type. Big gamer, tech wiz.
- Penny. Smartest of the group, but the least popular. Quiet, reserved and by far the nicest.

I was beginning to think we'd reached a dead end when Luca suggested halfway through the week that we take a break and go for an early morning run to clear our heads.

On Wednesday morning we sprinted to the woods just beyond the grounds. We practised self-defence and I expected Luca to be way ahead of me, but it was surprising how much of Iyabo's instruction had stayed with me. I managed to floor Luca a couple of times, and I could tell he was impressed.

'Iyabo's great, isn't she?' he said, as we jogged back to Sankt Hallvard Manor. 'An inspiring teacher.'

'Did she teach you too?' I stopped inside the gates to catch my breath, pausing to admire my trainers. Pity I couldn't send a picture of them to Vi; she'd know what a big deal they were for me.

'Yeah. She's brilliant.'

As I straightened up again, I was met with the sight of Luca's faded black T-shirt. It showed off his back, muscles rippling underneath. I felt heat in my cheeks and looked away, focusing on his ear instead, noticing the tiny hole where he'd removed his skull earring. Not for the first time since we'd arrived, I wondered who the *real* Luca was. Dark and brooding or easy and breezy—I couldn't decide.

'Anyway...' Luca lowered his voice, even though there was no one around. 'I've got some important intel.'

I adopted his hushed tones. 'I'm all ears.'

'Turns out Elliot is sneaking off at night, too. I've been fast asleep as soon as my head hits the pillow—until last night.'

'Really on the ball there then!'

He looked insulted. 'Everything's been so hectic—'

'Yeah, yeah, get on with it.' I felt a twinge of satisfaction that while Luca had been snoozing like a baby, I'd been on high alert, like a legit spy. The fact that I was a light sleeper had nothing to do with it!

He grinned. 'But last night, I woke up and noticed his empty bed. Must have been around midnight. I don't know how long he'd been gone, reckon I dozed off around 11 p.m. Did Beatrice disappear, too?'

'Er . . .' I stalled. 'For once, I slept heavily last night, so I'm not sure if she snuck out or not. But maybe . . .'

'They met up?' Luca looked thoughtful.

'So, maybe they've got a thing?'

'He likes her, but why not just hang out in plain sight, like normal people?' He grinned again. 'Like us, sweetheart.'

'Be serious! Why *are* they meeting up? How about tonight, I'll stay awake, but play dead. Hopefully, Bea will sneak out again, now that she reckons she put me off the scent with all the gym talk. And I'll find out what those two are up to.'

Luca nodded, smiling. I think I detected admiration at the way I'd taken control—felt pretty good to me.

Around 10 p.m. that night, I lay still in bed, though my breathing was so loud I was convinced Beatrice would demand to know why I was awake. I squeezed my eyes shut, listening for the click of the door being closed. And eventually, just like before, she crept out after her shower.

I pulled on a long dark jumper with pockets over my nightdress and put the USB stick in my pocket. I stuck my bare feet into my new trainers, glad they'd lost most of their squeak. My heart was banging— this was the most thrilling, maybe dangerous, thing that I'd done since I'd arrived.

Luca and I had monitored all five targets (including Penny) separately during the afternoon, and although they gathered often and had intense conversations, no one had gone anywhere or done anything to be suspicious about.

I opened the door slowly, wincing against the creaking. No sign of Beatrice. The landing lights were dim, but the fire exit sign above the stairwell glowed green, giving off enough light to see by.

At the bottom of the stairs, I caught a flash of Beatrice's white dressing gown. So she wasn't going to another girl's room. Maybe she was headed to the boys' rooms across the courtyard—did she and Elliot meet for some romantic alone-time?

Ewww. But there were cameras in all the communal areas, so where did they go where they wouldn't be monitored?

I crept along the corridor quietly, stopping every few feet. Reaching the main staircase, I noted the front door had been wedged open with a brick. Beatrice had gone outside.

The main lawn was surrounded by pine trees. To the left and right were science annexes. I caught sight of Beatrice darting off the side of the lawn, down a gravel path and towards a small block behind a science lab. I followed at a distance, but it was clear from her confident, speedy steps that she often made this journey. She wasn't being particularly careful, didn't glance behind her once.

I followed her inside the one-storey building and looked around. Doors lined the walls either side of a narrow metal staircase. I peered through the small glass partitions, but the rooms were dark, and the doors locked. Something sounding like metal clanged above me.

What was that? Where was Beatrice?

I headed for the staircase, but it didn't look like it led anywhere. Above it was a closed hatch, probably the roof. That had to be where Beatrice had gone though—there was nowhere else.

I pushed the hatch up and holding it open a fraction, squinted through. Beatrice, Ruby, Penny, and Jay were sitting on a blanket. I couldn't hear much, but I caught the words 'bitcoins' and 'permissions'.

'You lost?' said a voice.

I dropped the hatch with a bang. Elliot, the target I knew the least, was standing on the stairs right behind me, so close that I could feel his breath on my neck.

'Evidently, I'm not . . . lost.' I tried to smile.

Chill, Amber!

Nervous babbling would make me look guilty at best, and at worse . . . very uncool, so I waited. At training camp Iyabo said if you wanted information, the thing to do was to stay silent. Most people had an urge to fill silence. If Elliot just said something else . . .

The silence grew in intensity. He stared evenly at me before saying, 'No one likes being spied on.'

What the—

My heart thumped, and I clenched my jaw, hoping he wouldn't notice my hands shaking. I jammed one hand into my pocket and squeezed my fingers around the recording USB stick. All I had to do to activate it was slide it open. Could I do that one-handed . . .?'

Elliot's eyes narrowed suspiciously. My palms felt clammy and my armpits prickled with sweat.

'I'm not—'

'I'm kidding,' he said, laughing. 'Relax! Looking for someone?'

Relieved, I let out a nervous laugh myself. 'Yeah. I heard Beatrice get up and—well, I can't deny it—I was curious. Didn't want to miss out.'

'On what?'

'A party?' I said, shrugging. 'Isn't that what us . . . rich kids do after hours? Midnight feasts and all that?'

His jaw stiffened. 'A party?' He frowned; his tone became contemptuous. 'We're not stupid kids at some sleepover.'

'Well, I meant . . . you know, a *proper* party. Get-together. Whatever.'

'Sadly no. We're meeting for something altogether more . . . significant.' He swept the hair out of his eyes and grinned again, this time showing a tongue piercing I'd not noticed before. *Yowch!*

Right then, I knew I'd passed whatever his invisible test was.

'Come on, then. We'll see what the others say.'

He stood down a step to allow me to go up and

wiggle through the hatch.

As we clambered through, out onto the flat roof, the others turned around. Their smiles for Elliot dropped when they noticed me.

'*Amber?*' Bea said.

I channelled Luca's easy-going nature. 'Any biscuits left?' I wished he was here, but this was going OK; no one was waving a pitchfork or anything. *Not yet anyway.*

'What do you reckon?' Elliot asked, giving the others a pointed stare, his head tilted in my direction.

So was Elliot the real leader and not Beatrice? Why hadn't I picked up on that before? Maybe because I hadn't seen that much of him. But, clearly, his low profile was as much a cover as mine and Luca's fake romance.

'Wait,' he said, flicking his hand, indicating I should move away. He joined his friends on the blanket where they huddled together, whispering—about me, no doubt.

I used this as a chance to slide open the USB stick and hopefully the device was now recording whatever conversation happened.

Please say something incriminating.

After a few minutes, Beatrice beckoned me over. 'Alright, placement girl. Ruby says you're OK. You helped her in debate when she had a brain melt?'

I shrugged. 'No big deal.' Everything inside me went *Yessss!* Outwardly, I maintained composure by sticking my hands in my pockets, super casual.

'So, what do you do up here?' I asked, plonking myself next to Penny who looked pleased to see me. Then everyone started talking at once, and it was clear they'd been dying to share all this with *someone*.

'So,' Beatrice announced solemnly, as if she were royalty, 'we meet up once a week to discuss new projects that have come in. We're part of this exclusive—'

'Club,' Penny said, twisting her hands in her lap.

Ruby piped up, shaking her head. 'Not exactly—'

'I wouldn't describe it as that,' Jay said, tossing a handful of stones over the other side of the roof. 'We come here for *privacy*. It's the only place the security cameras can't access. Anyway, we're not a club, more like an . . . *elite network*.'

'Oh, OK. Like . . . a school thing?' I asked, intentionally sounding clueless. 'Is it political?

They looked at each other, wondering how to explain. Beatrice sighed and then said patronizingly, 'Amber. Do you have any idea what hacking is?'

'Duh!' Jay laughed. 'If she got into Sankt Hallvard Manor, then she has *skills*. Everyone knows what hacking is!'

Elliot snapped. 'No, they don't. In fact, most people don't have the first clue, if you must know. The word has been misused and thrown around: life hacks and blah, blah. Hacktivists—us—are highly skilled, with certain personality traits in common.'

Wow, this guy was in danger of vanishing up his own butt.

Even Penny frowned. Ruby nibbled her lip.

He carried on, sounding extremely pleased with himself. 'We might tamper with software or electronic systems to discover . . . new ways of working.'

'So, what or who are you hacking?' I asked, wide-eyed.

'We've done different projects,' Ruby said. 'Right now? We're part of this . . . dare game.'

'Like truth or dare?' I asked, winding Elliot up. Seeing his nostrils practically flare, I was relieved Luca wasn't here because I'd have laughed out loud by now.

Elliot threw his hands up and sighed, aggravated. 'No, not quite. We started off small, but we've been doing this for a while. We've hacked into school systems—found out test scores.'

Was that it? Big deal.

My face remained blank.

'But . . . lately, there's been . . . riskier stuff,' Ruby added, clearly trying to impress or shock me.

'Oh?' I leaned in, not giving anything away. 'Go on . . .'

Jay looked smug. 'Like, transferring money to and from banks.'

'Really?' I put just enough shock into my voice. *But seriously, were they stupid?* 'What's the purpose of moving the money?'

Penny said, 'Think of us like the digital version of Robin Hood.'

The others nodded, pleased with her analogy— and themselves.

'Like . . . oh my God, it's such fun!' Beatrice clapped her hands together.

Jay crowed, 'Apparently, we're the most innovative, original, adventurous, and creative minds they've ever seen!'

They?

Elliot elbowed Jay sharply in the ribs and he clamped his mouth shut. He had clearly been about to spill essential info.

'So, what do you get out of it?' I asked.

Penny was the only one who didn't sound patronizing when she said, 'Bitcoin.'

'It's not really about the money,' Elliot added. 'It's a challenge—seeing if we can beat the system.'

'Absolutely,' Beatrice added. 'And we do, most of the time.'

They plainly thought this was a great game. But from what Clara had said it was serious. Didn't they understand what they were doing had *real* consequences? Compromising computers and confidential systems was wrong and possibly dangerous—didn't they care? Were they only thinking of themselves?

Beatrice tossed her hair. 'What do you think?'

'Yeah, wow . . .' I trailed off, nodding, like I was chewing it over. I tried to think of what to say. How could I balance what I really thought and felt, with what *Spy* Amber might say? Should I ask to become a part of their group, or would that look suspicious?

I had it: flattery.

'Wow. You guys must be *amazing* with computers. That sounds complex, really . . . high level.' A cool breeze reminded me where we were and what time it was, and I shivered.

Suddenly, a light on the roof of another building across from us clicked on. *A timer?*

Penny glanced at her watch. 'We best head back,' she said.

Beatrice and I were the last ones down the staircase and I nearly tripped on the bottom step. She gripped my arm, wobbling herself.

'Too much to drink?' I joked.

Leaning on me, she said, 'I thought you were just one of those self-righteous noobs who'd get on their high horse. But you're . . . actually alright.' She bumped my shoulder with hers and I bumped back.

'Just one thing.' Beatrice whirled round and brushed my fringe out of my eyes. Her pointed nail trailed lightly against my cheek. 'If you ever breathe a word about what we talked about tonight you'll wish you'd never been born.' Her eyes bored into my mine.

She wasn't joking.

I managed not to flinch, even though my heart was pounding in my throat.

'As if.' I shook my head. 'You can trust me, Bea. I love what you guys are doing. I'd never betray you. Any of you.'

Her steely gaze stayed in place for a few seconds more, before she smiled, close-lipped.

'Come on, then. Race you back to the room,' she said lightly, as though she'd not just threatened me.

We tore back across the lawn, through the wedged-open front door, and ran up the stairs, taking them two at a time.

Beatrice hurled herself on her bed. Her eyes were sparkling and even though she was the enemy, her smile gave me a warm feeling inside. I'd made a friend!

Reality jolt: I'd made *pretend* friends. None of them knew the real me. This was simply step one to infiltrating and stopping whatever was going on. Instead of feeling high on this victory, I went to sleep with Vi on my mind. I missed my real friend, right now.

I missed her badly.

CHAPTER 19

For the next few days Beatrice was all over me, like I was her best friend. I'd reported to Luca what had happened and given him the USB to listen to—I could barely keep the grin off my face as I told him about my major spy breakthrough.

I was far from perfect of course, but I'd secured important, potentially game-changing information.

'Well done, Ambs. Nice job.' Luca had moved in for a congratulatory hug, which I wasn't expecting.

I was so used to Mum's constant hugs that two weeks without any hugs at all made me realize how much I missed the contact, even though I'd pushed her away lately. Mum. Dad. The Baby. Was it really going to be as bad as I thought?

'So.' Luca finally let go but stayed close. 'Make sure you keep in with them. If Bea treats you like her bestie, then go with it—that way, asking any "innocent" questions will get better results. Just keep playing the laid back, funny-girl card.' He paused and stared at me. 'You've got a great natural weapon at your disposal, Amber. Use it.'

'I'm funny?' I crossed my arms and tried not to grin from the buzz his words had given me. 'Aren't *you* the witty one around here?'

'There's room for two of us, I guess.' He beamed at me. 'A double act?'

Beatrice now insisted I should sit with her and Ruby at breakfast and when I walked into the dining room with her each day, I felt a foot taller. True, her conversation topics revolved around make-up and fashion, but everything was different—now that I'd been accepted by *all* the hackers. I didn't feel as self-conscious as before, or that I needed to prove myself.

As Beatrice chattered about the latest MAC lipstick with Ruby, I privately regrouped on mine and Luca's progress. We only had one more week at Sankt Hallvard Manor; this was our last Saturday. So far, we'd got familiar with the hackers, but had no clue who they were working for or with. Luca assured me that he was conducting his own investigation—'guy stuff'—and that it was better I didn't know everything right now.

'See, if I told you, I'd have to kill you,' he'd told me, smiling, and I couldn't help but notice how much I liked his smile, especially when it was directed at me. Bluey and Phonegate seemed like a year ago, although it was only three weeks since we'd first met.

Queueing at the food station at lunchtime, I noticed all five hackers huddled over a table. Elliot was talking animatedly, his hands making sweeping gestures *at* Penny, who looked intimidated in the face of what looked like an interrogation.

Beatrice appeared to be trying to quiet him down and keep Ruby and Jay from joining in.

I quickly heaped salad and a jacket potato onto my plate, sneaking glances their way—noticing Penny shrinking further into her seat.

'Amber!' she called out, raising her arm and waving me over. It looked almost like an SOS, like she was afraid of something.

I sat next to her but as soon as I did, the lively conversation faded. The atmosphere was tense.

While I ate, I caught Penny turning to face Jay. I stared straight ahead at a point on the wall, trying to focus on what they were saying, without looking like I was eavesdropping.

Penny's voice was gentle but determined. 'No, *I know*. But it's what *I*—'

'Look.' Elliot held up his hand, cutting her off. 'The information needs to be out there. And,' he lowered his voice, 'I intend to fix this.'

I leaned in closer.

Out of the corner of my eye I saw Penny press the heels of her hands into her eye sockets, as if warding off tears. 'You're not *listening*,' she said. 'I don't think it's right for you to—'

Elliot glared across the table, butting in. 'Penny. The fact is . . . we don't bloody care whether or not you help us out with this one. You've been . . . useful, but I know what I'm doing now.'

Uh-oh. Trouble in paradise.

'Yeah.' Beatrice leaned against Elliot's shoulder and snuggled up to his neck. 'Not to be harsh but . . . we *can* easily do this without your input.'

Penny blinked rapidly and mumbled, 'We said, when this started, that everyone should be on the same page. Staring hard at her plate, she swiped at her eyes.

Beatrice smiled over at me, and then she patted Penny's arm.

'Elliot doesn't *really* mean he doesn't care. This is a big deal to him, that's all.' Her eyes flicked to me and away again.

Penny glared at Beatrice, whimpered, and shoved her tray to one side. She pushed back her chair. 'I'll—I'll see you later,' she said, rushing out of the dining hall.

I took a long drink of squash, watching everyone's reactions over the rim of my glass. No one followed her. Ruby just muttered, 'Typical!'

Jay shook his head, sulking. 'Remind me why she's even involved again?' He turned to Beatrice. 'I knew she wouldn't get it.'

Wow. Harsh. They sounded more like Penny's enemies, not her friends. They might be clever, rich, and innovative, but without kindness, empathy, or loyalty, I wouldn't choose them as friends unless I had to. I wanted to run after Penny, but that might look suspicious, since we weren't particularly close. I waited a few minutes, before 'suddenly remembering' I needed something I'd left in our room and then I set off, leaving the others bickering.

Walking the corridors of Sankt Hallvard Manor, I thought of where I'd hide, if I was upset. It was raining, so outside wasn't an option. Then I remembered that Penny liked books, so maybe the library?

I was nearly there when Professor Ellery appeared

at the other end of the corridor.

I slowed my pace, adjusting my breathing, and gave her a broad smile as she sidled up alongside me.

'Ah. Miss De La Courte.' She smiled back. 'Where are you off to?'

'I'm heading to the library,' I said. 'Working on my debate techniques.'

'Excellent.' She glanced at my hands which I hadn't realized I was twisting together.

Rookie error: sign of anxiety.

'But, don't study so hard that you neglect your friends. I see you're mixing with the smart set. Is everything alright?' she asked. 'You look a little . . . frazzled.'

I put my hands on my waist, adopting a gung-ho position. 'Raring to go.'

'With the debate presentation homework?' She gave a strange laugh that sounded like a bark. 'Well, whatever floats your boat, as they say.'

'But . . .' I was confused. 'I thought you wanted me to improve.'

'I do. But you mustn't get too wound up about it. The point is to step back and think through your points. Forget you'll have an audience. Just focus on the information you want to get across. Keep your objective at the forefront of your mind. Always.'

'Thanks.' I glanced into the library. I needed to talk to Penny before she left. 'That's good advice.'

Professor Ellery sailed past me. 'Have a good afternoon.'

As I slid through the library doors, I glanced to my left to see her giving me a little wave. I'd bonded with a professor as well as the hackers; I was on a roll.

I couldn't spot Penny at first, but after I'd gone up and down a few aisles, my deductions proved correct.

Penny looked startled when I rounded a corner. She was sat with her back against a radiator, next to the history volumes. Although she hastily stuffed a tissue into her pocket, it was obvious she'd been crying.

'Penny. Everything alright?'

She sniffed. 'I don't think I want to do this any longer.'

I sat next to her. 'What?'

'This club, this hacking stuff.' She shook her head.

I decided to take a risk. 'It can't be *that* bad, can it? No harm is being done, is it?' I bit my tongue, wondering if I'd gone too far, but she just sighed.

'But that's the thing. I don't know how much

you know about hacking, but we can cause quite a lot of . . . damage. Every job pushes us further. They're all getting carried away and I don't think they understand the danger. Amber, if I tell you something—will you swear not to mention it to a living soul?'

I shrugged like this wasn't a big deal. 'Sure.'

'Elliot recruited us. He has the contact, although they're anonymous, so no one knows where the challenges come from. At first it was sort of . . . fun, and a good way of practising our computer skills. But, for a while now, every time a new project comes up, it's bigger and more intricate. And now, it's gone too far. It's getting nasty and things are becoming . . . *personal*. Elliot always swore it was only banks and social-media corporations, not actual people, but . . . lately, there's been mention of threats and the whole thing feels *wrong*. I don't know what to do.'

I desperately wanted to know what Elliot was doing and why. But asking those specific questions would be a massive red flag. I couldn't risk it.

'So . . . why don't you quit?' I said instead.

'What? And go back to having no friends and being on my own?' Penny nibbled her fingernails. 'Anyway. I just can't . . . it'd look weird. And if I tell anyone about the hacking, then they'll find out it was me.'

What should I say? Remembering Iyabo's advice, I stayed quiet and waited for Penny to reveal more.

It didn't take long. 'I'm good at programming. I liked sharing what I knew and, at first, the others seemed interested. Elliot's trying to gain unauthorized access to systems we shouldn't be tampering with, and he insists *we're* the good guys—white hats—breaking into systems and pointing out security flaws or bringing attention to causes that need it. But what's going on now isn't exactly that . . .'

I nodded and gave her a sympathetic look. 'And how did Elliot get involved?'

'He's a gamer. Jay says he cheats a lot, and in a chat room once, he ended up meeting some bigwig after boasting about his skills at getting other players kicked out.'

I felt sorry for her; she'd joined the group hoping to make friends who had similar interests and they'd basically just taken advantage of her.

The bell rang, shrill and loud, reminding us lunchtime was over.

Penny wiped her eyes. 'Sorry. I went on a bit. I-I'm probably being overdramatic. Forget it.' She stood up. 'Forget I said anything.'

'I don't think you're being dramatic. It sounds . . .

scary,' I said, putting my hand on her shoulder. 'Let's catch up after next lesson?'

'Thanks, Amber,' Penny said, smiling. 'It's been good having you here to talk to.'

We left the library together, and when Penny walked outside to get some fresh air, I stopped by the noticeboard. I wasn't interested in anything on it, I just needed some time to digest what she'd told me.

Luca appeared from nowhere, sidling silently up to me.

'Jeez!' I clutched my throat. 'You frightened me.'

'Sorry, practising my stealth moves.' He put his hands in his pockets.

'There's going to be a mutiny. Penny wants out . . .' I said, trying to keep the elation out of my voice. I took his arm, dragging him away from some girls who'd stopped to read about extra maths tuition, and led him outside to a science annex.

'OK, spill!' Luca smiled, making a gracious 'after you' gesture with a flourish.

'I don't know the details yet, but for Penny this latest hack is a step too far. She says it's *dangerous*. I'm hoping she'll confide more. I just need to get her complete confidence, and trust. I'm nearly there.'

'Better work fast, Amber. We haven't much time!'

The next day I had a pang of guilt—Penny trusted me, and I was passing information on, but I reminded myself that it was for the greater good. Passing on any information would protect Penny and everyone else in the long run.

Track was after lunch. I was looking forward to clearing my head with a run, though how much thinking I'd manage with Luca chatting away, I had no idea.

But at lunchtime, Luca shuffled towards me. As he came closer, I squinted. He had a black eye! His cheek was puffy and bruised too.

'What happened?' I exclaimed.

'Oh, this?' He pointed to his face and shrugged sheepishly. 'You know, just got into a little scuffle.'

'Luca!'

He leaned in close. 'Elliot had a swipe at me.'

'What? Why?' Oh God, please don't tell me Elliot had found the USB stick.

'Last night, I was searching through his bag, trying to find evidence. He'd gone to Jay's room, but he came back for it and caught me.'

'Jeez. Does he suspect anything?'

'No, no. It's just . . . he definitely doesn't trust me now, that's for sure. I said I was looking for chewing gum, but he didn't believe me and we kind of got into it. Anyway, forget it. Come on, let's run.'

We completed a 400-metre lap of the track, and soon, we were running together, far ahead of everyone else. Just like running with Vi, it felt easy and comfortable. We needed the exercise, apart from how important it was for our mission to have some private time with no one else nearby. Both of us were aware that time was running out. We only had five more days to crack this operation.

As we stretched out, Luca gave me a pep talk. A fortnight ago I'd have found that infuriating, but at this stage I needed it. I wanted to get this right.

'You know what you need to focus on?' Luca bent over to touch his toes.

'Gaining Penny's trust,' I said.

'Yep. Because she's *nice*. She wants to do the right thing and serious doubt has set in about her teammates. She's chosen you as her confidante, which gives you power, Amber. The Agency already know who the hackers are, right? But we need more. We need evidence of who recruited Elliot, details of the jobs they've been doing, and what they're up to next.'

'Right.' I bit my lip.

You've got this, Amber.

First, I had to try and prepare for the debate

presentation tomorrow. I just wanted it out of the way. I'd spent time perfecting and revising my arguments and presentation, but I didn't know if it was enough.

It should be fine. Debating skills weren't really what I was here for, I told myself. But still, now that I knew what achievement felt like, I didn't want to fail any aspect of this mission.

'Better go,' I said. 'I'll find Penny and get what we need.'

'Good luck.' Luca grinned. 'You're killing it, Amber.'

The next bell sounded. On my way to HTML class, Penny was coming down the stairs from the bedrooms. Alone.

Now was my chance.

When she got to the bottom of the stairs, I gently touched her elbow. 'You alright?'

She nodded, though her eyes were red-rimmed.

I said, 'I think . . . I can help you, with this group hacking thing, if you're uncomfortable and want out.'

She looked hopeful but wary, too. 'Really? How?'

'If there are, you know, things you don't want to get involved in, I know someone who can take a closer look, see how serious it is—what Elliot's been doing.'

'Who?'

'Someone . . . neutral who understands tech stuff. They don't know who you are.'

She frowned. 'Maybe . . . But absolutely no one else can know, Amber. If we're found out, then . . .' She chewed her upper lip and wrapped her arms around herself protectively. 'We'll be in so much trouble.'

I touched her hand. 'Look. *You* won't be. Whistle-blowers are protected. The fact that you've done the right thing . . . that counts for a lot.'

'I don't know.' She looked terrified. 'I'm worried!'

'Penny. Trust me.' I paused. I couldn't give myself away. I couldn't let Penny know that I was a spy and my boss would take care of it. I had to think of something else. 'You could be an anonymous source. I won't tell my friend who you are, or anything about you. It's completely safe.'

'Promise?' She suddenly looked like a kid.

'Pinky promise.' I linked her little finger in mine and felt a burst of genuine affection and concern. 'I hate seeing you in bits about this.'

She smiled as we squeezed pinkies. 'Thanks, Amber. You're the only one who cares about how

I feel. The others think I'm a loser, I know that. I'm not stupid.'

'They're not as brave as you.'

'OK, what do you want me to do?' She stood up straighter and I realized that she'd made up her mind.

'Can you get proof of the dares you've been doing onto a memory stick—emails, screengrabs, that sort of thing?'

'I think so, yes,' she said. 'I can do that. I *will* do that. After all, a robot—or a human—must protect its own existence. Correct?'

'That's the spirit,' I said, grinning. 'Leave it with me. You do your bit, get me that stick, and I'll do mine.'

CHAPTER 20

I couldn't believe this afternoon was the Big Debate—in front of the entire school—and my class was up next. I'd had three debate lessons and studied techniques every spare moment, but I still wasn't fully prepared.

Most of my class was already on stage. The rest of the school filed noisily into the main hall. I was in the middle of a throng moving extra slowly, waiting for Penny to pass me the memory stick we'd discussed yesterday. Suddenly, an elbow nudged me in the back.

'Here you go,' Penny whispered, pushing something into my hand. 'Take it!' Just as my fingers touched the stick, she swerved left, deep into the crowd.

OK. I had it. A memory stick with everything

she knew. Penny had stuck to her word, but now I needed to get up on stage and debate with my classmates. I didn't have anywhere to put the stick! My trouser pockets were sewn shut, which I hadn't realized until just now.

Grrr. Stupid trousers.

Thankful, finally, for being so tall, I looked over everyone's heads and spotted Luca by the hall doors. Could I get the USB stick to him? I dropped back, letting people shuffle and push past me, and ducked away from Elliot who was heading straight in my direction. I dodged backwards until I almost stepped on Luca's foot and watched the crowd swallow Elliot up.

'Aren't you supposed to be up there?' He pointed at the stage. 'I'm looking forward to this.'

'Haha, funny. Look, Penny gave me this.' I opened my fist, showing him the USB stick.

'Nice work!'

'Think you can, you know, get it to The Agency?'

'I'll do my best,' he said, pocketing it. We grinned at each other and it felt, right then, as if we were the perfect team. If it hadn't have looked weird, I'd have reached out for a high-five.

'Shame I'll miss your big moment though.' His eyes twinkled. 'Good luck! You'll be great.'

As the audience surged forward into their seats, Luca eased backwards through the main doors, giving me a thumbs up. I turned to face the stage—I had to get up there—and glimpsed Penny, a few feet away, glowering.

'*What the*—?' she mouthed, furious.

I shook my head frantically, trying to indicate everything was fine, that it wasn't whatever she thought it was.

It was worse, actually, but not for her. Not if she wanted out.

'Don't worry!' I mouthed back, but her grimace didn't fade. But I couldn't do anything to reassure her right now.

I climbed up on stage to join the rest of my debate class, sitting on a chair in the row facing the audience.

My hands were so sweaty. Where was Professor Ellery? She swore she'd be with us every step of the way. I wanted her support. She'd been so helpful, taking time to give me extra pointers, taking a special interest. My stomach was jittery; I should have eaten more at lunch, or . . . maybe less?

I'd rehearsed my debate speech in front of Beatrice *and* the mirror many times already, but five hundred students staring at me was the most intimidating thing I'd ever faced. This would be hideous.

In the audience the front row jostled each other, getting settled. Penny stared daggers at me. I chewed my lip, trying to direct a reassuring smile her way, but she wasn't having it. Fire burned in her eyes.

As soon as it was over, I'd go down and apologize. She must have seen me give the USB stick to Luca— my 'boyfriend', hardly the expert I'd promised. Maybe . . . I could lie and claim that the tech expert was a friend of his? It still didn't look good, though.

I closed my eyes. *Not now, Amber.* No time to freak out. I needed to channel everything— anything—I'd learnt into a focused debate. I needed to speak slowly, take pauses, remember to breathe and project my voice.

Not too hard, right? Amber De La Courte, you can do this.

Be calm. *Fake it till you make it!*

The debate subject was the ethics of surveillance. I'd rehearsed the key arguments in my mind for days. Talk about the universe joking at my expense, huh?

Ruby dusted herself down and stepped up to the microphone. She cleared her throat. This first round she was debating *for*, and I was debating for the opposition. She directed a winning smile around the hall.

Everyone hushed.

Luca would pass The Agency the info, and then this would be over. I'd be home safely in three days.

Home.

Just . . . this little debate to get through first. I breathed in slowly and deeply through my nose and out through my mouth.

'We need to be kept safe; wouldn't you agree?' Ruby began.

I tuned in and out of her telling us how unsafe the world was these days. *Duh!* We knew those facts; they were plastered daily over the news. Ruby spoke well though.

'If you've nothing to hide then why worry about being monitored?' she asked, rhetorically. Rhetoric was one of debate's strongest tools.

I'd debated with Ruby a few times now, and it was easy to tell when she was gearing up to deliver her big conclusion.

'And being monitored works!' she declared, with a flourish. Everyone applauded. Still no sign of Professor Ellery. Where *was* she?

Mr Jones, evidently asked to step in at the last minute, examined his clipboard. 'For the opposition, Amber De La Courte!'

His tone was too enthusiastic, like we were in

a talent show. I stepped up to a microphone and composed myself. The bad news: every time I looked out into the front row, I glimpsed someone I knew: Elliot, Penny, and Jay all peered at me, waiting.

'We need to be kept free!' I announced.

Good opener. Nice one, Amber.

'Constant monitoring doesn't work,' I continued. 'People don't feel they're being trusted if they're being spied on—ask any teenager!'

Ripples of laughter.

I stared across to the teachers lining the walls. My mouth went dry. My gaze rested on the back doors which had suddenly opened.

Luca stood in the doorway and I could see, even from this distance, that he was *not* happy. His curls were wild and sticking up, like he'd been running his hands through them, and his expression looked pained.

What had happened? Had he lost the memory stick?

He moved his hand wildly at his side, like paddling without oars. What was he trying to say?

He looked really agitated, not at all like his usual cool self.

I fumbled, and the audience tittered because, distracted by Luca's flapping hand, I'd dried up and had stopped talking completely. I looked at my classmates and they stared back with *what-the-hell* expressions.

Mr Jones said, 'Miss De La Courte? We're waiting.'

My cheeks flamed. What had I been saying? I gaped at Mr Jones, searching his face for an answer, and he whispered loudly, 'Continue!'

Oh, yes. Right. What had I been saying?

But Luca widened his eyes like a cartoon character, eyebrows waggling, his hand summoning me. He jiggled about impatiently. I'd never seen him like this.

I had to go! *Now.*

I shrieked, 'Free speech!' like a maniac, fluttered my eyelids as if I was going to faint, and dramatically clamped a hand over my mouth. I lurched forward and tripped, which, frankly, only made my performance more convincing, then rushed off stage towards the back doors; flapping my hand and making the teachers flinch—looking like I was going to projectile vomit any second.

CHAPTER 21

As I hurtled through the hall doors, Luca grabbed my hand, and we ran together.

'We need to get out of here, fast!' he roared.

We tore down the corridor, past the dining hall, and burst out through the main entrance.

'What's happened? Where are we going?' I panted; thankful I was wearing trainers.

'The upload was intercepted!'

'What does that mean?'

'It means I couldn't get any info to The Agency— someone stopped the program, *as* it was running. From the inside! We've underestimated that lot. Someone's onto us. My suitcase has been searched; my stuff was everywhere. We need to go!'

'But we're in the middle of nowhere!'

Luca stopped halfway down the lawn. No one

was behind us, but he looked freaked out, his eyes wild—he was shaking.

'Listen, I can't explain—just trust me! We could be in danger. I don't think anyone is following us *yet*, but I can't be sure. Stay close.'

'Where can we go?' I tried not to panic.

'Head for the bike sheds, and then we'll get out of the grounds.'

Now that we were standing still, holding hands felt super weird, so I wriggled out of his grasp. He jogged on, and I followed, past the car park and to the bike sheds.

'Ready for the run of your life?' Luca asked.

'You what?'

'We've got around two miles to cover. Like you said, we're in the middle of nowhere. Farmland everywhere with hardly any cover. The quicker we get moving, the better.'

I settled into a comfortable pace and pretended Vi and I were on the school track. Behind me, Luca's feet slapped the path leading out of the grounds.

Soon, we were deep in the vast Norwegian countryside. Apart from a few brick-coloured farmhouse buildings, all around were tall skinny trees, bordering open fields with cows grazing.

There was so much brilliant blue sky and if I hadn't been worrying about who we were running from, and where we were running to, then it would have been a relaxing cross-country route.

After twenty minutes, Luca suddenly swerved left into a row of hedgerows. I stopped, glad of a breather.

He rummaged deep in the bushes, parting leaves, until he emerged pushing a futuristic, very sleek-looking moped.

'What the heck?' I shrieked. 'A moped going fifteen miles an hour won't get us far!' I almost laughed because the idea of us on that contraption was ridiculous.

'This isn't just any moped, Amber,' Luca said. 'It's *driverless.*'

'You what?'

He cleared away the leaves and twigs from the wheels. 'This is The Agency's safety net. They told you they had something in place, right? Although things can get scary, Clara tries to avoid *too* much life-threatening danger, if she can help it.'

'You knew about this bike all along?' I asked, annoyed that I hadn't been told about it.

He shrugged and dived back into the bush for something else. 'I guess I'm in a position where I might not . . . freak out when things get a bit . . . dangerous?'

'I'm *not* freaking out!'

He emerged with a big bag and took out two helmets. 'You *seem* pretty freaked out. Look, Clara thought that the fewer people who knew about the moped the better. One less thing to keep secret.'

'Hmm. I suppose that makes sense,' I said, grudgingly.

'OK. Hop on, hold on, and let's go!'

'Is it safe, though?'

Luca sighed—a massive sigh, like the ones Mum sometimes directed at me. 'Seriously, Amber. You're worried about being safe, right now? Being a *spy* isn't safe. Anyway, this bike is our only friend, our *safest* option. It's an *electric* moped. Self-driving and pre-programmed to take us to a certain location. Honestly, I've been on these before, they're amazing. Quiet and perfectly reliable. Get on!'

Did I have a choice?

Handing me a helmet, Luca fiddled underneath the bike to press the start button. Once he was astride the bike, I got on behind him. I thought it'd feel wobbly, but the two wheels were wider than any I'd ever seen, so the base felt solid.

Luca put on his own helmet. 'This gets up some

speed, so hold onto me tight, OK?'

I put my hands lightly either side of his waist. Before I could deliver a comeback, the bike jolted forwards with a whirring noise like a malfunctioning microwave. It wobbled terrifyingly, and I closed my eyes and squeezed Luca hard, yelping, before the bike righted itself.

'Don't worry,' Luca said. 'The bike's just calibrating our weight.'

The bike accelerated fast; I had no idea what speed we were going.

We couldn't speak, not only because of the helmets, but because the wind whipped our words away. Although it was an incredible way to travel, it was hard trying to catch my breath.

The narrow road was straight, which was great, because I didn't fancy leaning to go around any corners. We put a good distance between us and Sankt Hallvard Manor. For all I knew, everyone was still busy debating.

We picked up more speed, and the road gave way to more of a dirt track. Just up ahead, branches were scattered on the surface and the bike leaned perilously over, as we skidded through some cow dung. The next thing we knew, we were hurled sideways onto the ground, crashing into a ditch as the bike carried on going.

I rolled along, twigs and gravel shredding my clothes, sharp rocks scraping my shoulders.

My helmet bounced and smacked against the ground, thankfully protecting my head. I tumbled three or four more times; kicking up dust. I squinted through my visor. *Where was Luca?* I saw him a few metres away, lying face down. His leg looked twisted. It took me ages to shuffle towards him.

Sitting up, I took off my helmet and winced at the pain shooting through my shoulder. I put my hand tentatively on his back.

'Luca?' My heart was in my throat. *No!* He couldn't be dead! I'd never seen a dead body and I didn't want him to be my first. If he was seriously hurt—what would I do? Who could I call? Did anyone know where I was?

As my tears hovered, Luca's ankles twitched. He slowly rolled onto his back. Relieved, I let out a little sob and helped him remove his helmet.

'What a ride!' He sat up, trying to grin.

I swatted his arm, harder than I meant to. 'You freakin' kidding me?'

'Yeah, kinda,' he said with a cough. He tried to stand, but his knee buckled, and he tipped over, grabbing me for support. '*Ow!* I've definitely ruined something. *You* OK?'

My top was ripped at the shoulder and blood seeped through the material. 'Oh!' I gasped. I hadn't felt much pain before—probably the adrenaline—but now that I saw a deep cut with flaps of stinging skin, I felt quite sick.

'Help me up?' he asked.

Standing, I bent over and Luca wrapped an arm around my waist. I hoisted him to his feet, and he winced. 'My duck and roll technique plainly needs work.'

I didn't laugh. Maybe Luca was just trying to keep our spirits up, but from where I stood, things looked hopeless. There really wasn't much to laugh about.

'*Now* what do we do?' I moaned.

'All is not lost.' Luca pointed towards the field's entrance. 'See over there?'

'What am I looking for?' I muttered.

'We *were* heading for the field on the other side of this track. You'll see. Come on, someone's waiting.'

With Luca leaning on me, hobbling together, we gradually made our way across the track and into a field opposite where there was a tiny white biplane.

'Is that ours?' I asked, hardly daring to believe it.

Luca nodded with his eyes half-closed, grimacing. 'You OK?'

'I'll live.' He smiled.

Crossing the field and finally reaching the plane, I helped Luca climb up the steps. 'Is Clara here?'

He tried to shake his head and ended up biting his lip. He gripped the back of the seat so hard that his knuckles went white. He was obviously in a lot of pain.

'Don't tell me this plane is driverless too!' I joked, hoping to raise a smile.

Luca had turned very pale. I hoped a first-aid kit was on board, or that there was someone to help him.

'Hello?' I shouted.

A cream curtain at the front flapped and a muffled male voice hollered, 'Strap yourselves in!'

That must be the pilot. I didn't recognize the voice.

Were we flying to meet someone, or were The Agency already on board? There were seats for four passengers, two sets of two with a narrow aisle separating them. I helped ease Luca into a seat and did up his belt.

Luca closed his eyes and slumped against the window, breathing shallowly. Perhaps he'd broken his ankle, or badly sprained it. I strapped myself in next to him.

The engine started. The plane taxied across the field and I braced myself for take-off. I leaned back against the seat in relief. This would all be over soon.

Once we were in the air, the curtain separating us from the front cabin jerked open.

I frowned, unable to place the woman standing in front of me.

Then it hit me.

'Professor Ellery!' I gasped.

'Hello.' She smiled, clasping her hands behind her back. 'How lovely to see you again.'

I elbowed Luca, but he was asleep, or maybe had lost consciousness. Thank God our safety net was here. *Wow*. The Agency had people everywhere! No wonder she'd been so interested in keeping an eye on me.

'The *debate* went well,' I babbled, stupidly thrilled to see an adult. 'Why weren't you there?'

'The . . . what?' She stared at me as if I was mad.

'The debate. I kept looking out for you. Do you know where the first-aid kit is? Luca's really hurt. Look.'

She frowned at me. 'Are you feeling quite alright?'

'Yes! *Yes*. I am *now*. Now that we're safe. Thank you. It's so reassuring that you're a part of it.'

'A part of what?'

'*Us*, The Agency!'

'Oh.' She pressed her lips together to stop herself from laughing. 'You're far from safe . . .'

Her smile was beginning to creep me out.

I shook my head. 'No?' My voice trembled. Out of the corner of my eye, all I could see was bright blue sky.

Professor Ellery brought a gun out from behind her back and pointed it right at me.

A GUN! Was that real . . .?

'Does this look *safe* to you?'

CHAPTER 22

'What are you doing?' I stuttered, my stomach plummeting.

If Professor Ellery *wasn't* working for The Agency, that meant she was our enemy, working for someone else! My head swirled.

Luca—wake up!

Gesturing with the gun, she smiled as if delivering good news. 'I hope not to use this, as long as you and your boyfriend cooperate.' She sat down and put her lap belt on.

'He's not my boyfriend!' Luca's eyes were closed, although his chest was moving, so he was still with us. I might have stood a chance against Ellery if Luca was conscious, because one of us could distract her, but without him? What could I do with a gun aimed at me?

Professor Ellery coughed. 'Pass me that water bottle.' She pointed to my armrest where a bottle of water lay. Picking it up, I wondered if I threw it, could I hit her? It might make her drop the gun, but would I be quick enough to reach it?

She must have read my mind. 'Don't get any silly ideas. Here. Throw it over!'

I threw the bottle gently over to her and she caught it one-handed, her eyes never leaving me.

Twisting the top off, she glugged the contents.

'The hackers' little club was my idea. My project,' she began. 'Remarkable how eager to please clever children are; desperately competitive to be the best and the brightest. Trusting, greedy, and too conceited to see the bigger picture, they'll fall for anything, especially flattery!'

Here she gave a Bond-villain cackle. 'I've had that group hacking people you'd never imagine! The lengths they went to in order to impress me, and outdo each other, were truly outstanding.'

OK. *Amber, stay calm. Focus.* I needed hard facts, in case I ever escape.

'Like what?'

Ellery studied her fingernails, nonchalantly. 'Deleting records of the FBI's most wanted criminals, for a fee, of course. Stealing money from trust funds and transferring the funds elsewhere. Creating chaos is CHAOS's job! Is it making sense yet, Amber? Why do you think I made you debate surveillance? We're trying to make people realize that nothing is secure or guaranteed, that way they're more vulnerable to suggestion.'

I nudged Luca, noticing that the colour had returned to his cheeks. *Please, Luca—wake up! Tell me you're hearing all of this!*

'The chaos is building, exactly like we wanted. But you two busybodies need to disappear. Before you do, I think you should see the consequences of your actions, so we're just taking a quick detour.'

'Where?'

'We're about to fly over Sankt Hallvard. And when we do, I'm going to detonate a device, hidden under the stage, which will blow the school sky high.'

'You can't do that! Hundreds will die!'

'That's exactly why we *are* doing it. Here's a debate topic for you: is it ethical to kill a few in order to save the many? We think so. None of us are safe. Especially the precious offspring of the wealthiest and most powerful people in Europe. All of whom are at that school!'

The plane had been smoothly cruising, but

suddenly it sloped left. I leaned over Luca to look out of the window. Ellery was right; the turrets of Sankt Hallvard Manor were coming into view.

Groans came from Luca's direction and his eyelids fluttered.

'Ooh, is lover boy waking up?'

I didn't have any weapons and had no idea if Luca would be able to fight. The time had come for less talking and more . . . getting out of this. I pinched the back of Luca's hand to hurry him along. The only way we'd overpower this lunatic was by working together.

Ellery held aloft a smartphone. 'Just one press of the button on my phone and . . . boom.'

'What the—?' Luca muttered, opening his eyes and shaking his head. He struggled upright, looking at us and the gun. 'Um, I take it *she's* the bad guy?' he whispered.

Ellery undid her lap belt and stood up, moving towards Luca.

Remembering Iyabo's training, I lurched out of my seat, and threw a direct punch at Ellery's throat. She wheezed, clutched her windpipe and dropped the gun. As she stumbled between the seats, trying to get her balance, I nudged Luca, waggling my wrist. My glittery, pink watch. *The EMP disruptor!*

Finally, Luca's gaze landed on it too and his eyes widened. I swivelled round, mouthed *'the watch'* and he beamed, giving me an almost imperceptible nod.

Clara told us that activating this watch would cut out anything electromagnetic. Ellery wouldn't be able to trigger the bomb, but . . . the plane might *also* malfunction.

But we had no other choice.

Luca tightened his lap belt and I sat back down and tightened mine.

I pressed the button on my watch.

As the plane skewed, I snatched Luca's hand. Ellery, still trying to reach her seat, dropped her phone. She leant over to pick it up, pressing buttons and scowling.

Had it worked? Was her phone now useless?

The plane dropped slightly and an eerie silence hummed as the engines cut out altogether.

Suddenly, the plane tilted, picking up speed. Luca and I jerked forward, the lap belt cutting into my thighs.

Ellery was thrown to the floor. She rubbed her forehead, looking confused. 'What's happening?'

After wobbling, the plane evened out. *Could the pilot fly with no electronics? What did autopilot do?* I wished I knew more about planes, electronics, and

. . . everything!

A yell came from the pilot behind the curtain. 'We're going down!'

'Brace for impact!' Luca shouted, grasping my hand. We pressed ourselves far back into the seats.

What was the proper brace position? Head between knees and hands over the top, protecting the skull. We were doing it wrong!

My stomach dropped. Was this it, was I going to die before I'd really lived?

Ellery was still kneeling on the floor, staring in a daze at her phone.

'It's not safe, get into your seat!' I roared.

Colour drained from her face and she stood, staggering towards a seat.

Suddenly, the plane rocked and dipped. My stomach dropping, I squeezed Luca's hand and shut my eyes, waiting for the crash.

CHAPTER 23

My ears were ringing, and although my eyes were closed, they stung like crazy. I couldn't move my neck. I touched my fingertips to it gently, and they came away sticky. *Blood?*

I stayed still. *Think.*

The last thing I remembered was the plane hitting the ground, but somehow I was alive. *Not dead.* That was good. Being alive was positive, right? And although I was confused, with my eyes shut, and smoke and heat clogging my throat, I wasn't brain dead either, since I was, you know, *thinking*.

Luca?

So, *not* brain dead, and . . . I wiggled my toes and then my legs, trying to process what had happened . . . not paralysed.

Jeez! I'd been in a plane crash.

'Amber? *Amber!* Are you alright?' Luca's voice was high and he sounded on the verge of tears. I opened my eyes gingerly, worried about what I'd see.

'You're laughing?! Why are you *laughing*? Have you lost your bloody mind?' Luca frowned as he struggled to release my lap belt. 'Very strange.' He waved away smoke with his hand, and I started coughing.

'Has to be hysterics—delayed shock, or whatever,' I replied.

'Whatever.' Luca prised the buckle apart and I twisted myself free.

Where was Professor Ellery, or the pilot? Would a gun be pressed against my head or back any minute?

'Ellery wasn't strapped in,' said Luca, looking around. 'She must be . . .'

He got up and we both moved towards the flapping curtain, but there was no sign of her. Luca bent over the pilot's body and took his pulse, then turned to me. 'He's just unconscious, but, you know, we probably don't want to hang around?'

'I guess not.' I shuddered.

Luca closed the curtain separating us from the cockpit.

He reached into an overhead compartment and took out a thick tartan blanket.

'What's that for?' I croaked, my throat dry and sore.

'It's for you; you're in shock. Most younger recruits don't last beyond one job,' he said, sighing, as he gently placed the blanket around my shoulders. He sounded sad. 'People join The Agency thinking the job will be all cool gadgets and exotic places, but after they've seen a few dead bodies—even though Clara provides counsellors—you can't really blame them when they quit.'

He gently took my hand in his and my fingertips tingled. 'Gets kind of . . . lonely,' he added, softly.

A smashed-up mobile lay on the floor. I knelt and pocketed it. Wherever Ellery was, she'd left behind her greatest weapon.

'How could Ellery just have vanished?' I said.

Luca blinked. 'Who knows.'

Limping, he led us out of the smoking plane, into the fresh air. We looked around us.

JEEZ! The plane had hit a tree virtually head on. Broken branches littered the windscreen and one wing was cracked. Thick, black smoke poured from the bent tail.

'Now what?' I shivered slightly, probably from the shock of realizing what a narrow escape we'd had.

Luca dug around in his waistband and removed four small sections of plastic, the size of credit cards. Slotting them together, he made the smallest mobile I'd ever seen.

'I'll call the bomb threat in, so that the school can evacuate.'

Five hours later, we were both back at The Agency's underground training camp, freshly showered and dressed in jumpsuits. I had a million questions, but after being checked by the medics, and having our cuts and bruises treated, Clara demanded we rest. She said everything could wait until our full debrief the next morning.

'We know more about CHAOS and their activities now, thanks to the two of you,' she said, once we were settled in a conference room. I wasn't interested in the plate of Hobnobs on the table though—I wanted answers.

'What *is* CHAOS exactly? What do they *want?*'

'Why, they want to *cause* absolute chaos of course, and then to pick up the pieces afterwards for their own gains.' Clara leaned forward, elbows on the table, and steepled her fingers under her chin. 'They're fed up of the world, they want to disrupt and destroy everything if they need to. They believe that people are fundamentally bad, and that individual liberty will lead to the disintegration of society.' She stared at us for such a long time that Luca started nudging my knee.

'We must monitor CHAOS closely to discover their next move. We have your USB stick, which, thankfully, due to Luca's quick thinking, hasn't been corrupted, and we can recover data from Ellery's smashed phone.'

'What happened to her?' I asked. 'She just . . . vanished.'

'We can't be sure, but I doubt that's the last we'll see of her.'

'And . . . what about everyone else?'

'Penny will be exonerated from any punishments that are given to the others. Their activity was criminal so there will be repercussions, although they'll avoid prosecution due to their ages. Your identities remain undetected. And from Luca's reports, I'm impressed with how you worked together. Amber, how did you find your first experience of espionage?'

My mind flicked back to the dining hall on the first day and meeting our targets. How out of my depth and strange I had felt, but then how satisfying it had been, winning Beatrice over and gaining

Penny's trust . . .

'*Different.* To begin with it was difficult pretending to be someone else, but then . . . yeah, I kind of got into it.'

'We don't have many spies your age who are as . . . adaptable. The way you embraced the assignment and extracted information from such a tightly knit group was remarkable.'

Luca nodded. 'It truly was.'

How did Clara know all this? 'Were you watching us?'

'No. But Luca filled me in occasionally, from a secure location.' Clara pressed buttons on a screen embedded in the table. 'Let's order you a hot chocolate.'

Luca grabbed two Hobnobs and crammed one into his mouth, whole. 'Someone's expecting me so are we done here? Iyabo said she can give me a lift. That alright, Boss?'

Boss?

'Of course, off you trot,' Clara said, waving Luca away. 'Keep your phone with you and we'll be in touch with details of your next assignment. That goes for you too, Amber.'

Next assignment?

A buzzer sounded. Clara clicked open a wall

panel and took out a mug of hot chocolate heaped with whipped cream, mini marshmallows, and a flake. *Mmm.*

I sipped it, cream attaching itself to my top lip at the exact moment Luca stood up with his hand held out for me to shake. 'Great getting to know you, Amber.'

I stared at his hand, the same one I'd held, squeezed and grabbed over the past forty-eight hours. My cheeks blared hot. We shook hands and he smiled, those dimples dimpling.

'For a newbie, you pick things up pretty fast.'

'Ha. Thanks.' I nibbled the inside of my cheek. It felt weird for him to just . . . leave like this. 'Good working with you.'

Oh, Amber! Is that the best you can do?

For three weeks, we'd spent every day together, yesterday we'd *virtually died* and yet, I had no idea if I'd ever see him again!

'See ya,' he said with a smile, walking out of the door. I almost expected him to add 'kiddo' but thankfully, he didn't.

'Bye.'

CHAPTER 24

Alexei handed me my real luggage as I got out of the car.

I dragged my case through the front gate, smiling as I spotted Mum in the doorway.

'Darling!' Mum yelped. 'She's back!'

Dad appeared right behind her, grinning. He'd taken the afternoon off. For me! It was so good to see them.

Clara had explained that The Agency had sent my parents an email regarding a 'minor injury', which explained my arrival home three days before the placement was due to officially finish—and my sling, of course.

Mum stood back, smiling, and I suddenly saw her stomach. *Wow.* It had grown! Seeing a proper bump was weird.

I reached out and put my hand on her tummy. She put her hand over mine and her eyes filled with tears.

'You'll always be my girl,' she whispered.

Tears prickled my own eyes. After spending the last three weeks in a strange place, dealing with hackers, a crazy professor, pretending to be someone else and hiding every real feeling I had—it was great to be home. *More* than great. Spending so much time out of my comfort zone had made me realize that having a new brother or sister wasn't that big a deal in the scheme of things. It might even be pretty cool.

Dad stepped forward and went in for a hug.

'Watch the sling, Dad!'

'We've missed you, sweetheart. The place wasn't the same without you—too quiet and too tidy! And no one to watch cheesy action films with, either.' He took my case off me.

What an awesome welcome home. I should go away more often.

'We've made your favourite for dinner.' Dad propped the case against the stairs and Mum groaned, 'Have you brought me three weeks' worth of laundry?'

'It's clean! The school had a laundry service.'

In the kitchen I took a deep breath, my nostrils flaring with the anticipation of spag bol later.

Mum put an apron over her head and tied it round

the back. 'I've asked Vi over for dinner, if that's alright?'

'Great!'

I was dying to speak to Vi. I could maybe even tell her about Luca, sort of, in code? And, as for her budding friendship with Taylor? Well . . . I'd need to act surprised, like I hadn't already seen her HappySnap account, but I could let that one go—I was home now. Everything was going to be fine. Life could just get back to normal.

At the kitchen table, Mum poured me a lemonade. 'You're not *too* upset about having to come home early, are you?'

'Definitely not.'

One hundred per cent the truth.

'School isn't expecting you back until Monday, so now you've got a few days off. You can relax at home.'

I gazed around the kitchen, appreciatively. Being home felt . . . different, somehow. Comforting. Maybe going away meant I could see more clearly what I had. I felt a stirring of excitement about the upcoming renovations. *Big changes. Challenges.*

'Has any building work started?'

Dad shook his head. 'Not yet, though we've found a builder who'll start soon. With your mum nearly four months gone, it's about time.'

'Absolutely,' I replied. 'Mum, can we have a shopping day together soon, to get stuff for the baby, if you haven't already?'

In my room, unpacking my clothes that I'd never even worn, Dad bellowed up the stairs.

'Amber! Vi's here!'

Vi! I nearly fell over rushing downstairs.

When I got to the bottom step, Vi was hanging up her coat. She turned around and we grinned at each other, a little shyly.

'What have you done to your hair?' I said. The ends of Vi's long, blonde hair were tinted purple.

'Like it?' She struck a pose, tossing her hair around.

'Looks great,' I said. 'Permanent?'

'*Ohmigod*, no way, are you kidding? Mum would *freak.*'

'Shame. It suits you.'

And just like that, any shyness between us vanished and it was as if I'd never gone away.

'What happened?' she asked, pointing at my sling.

'Oh, nothing really. Sprained my shoulder, tripped on the running track.'

She ruffled my hair. 'Stumbling over your own feet again, Big Bird?'

I laughed. 'I missed you,' I told her. 'I really did.'

'Me too, Amber. I mean, I missed you.' Vi reached out and hugged me tight, which hurt, but felt amazing at the same time.

Bolognese was already in bowls on the table and the smell of garlic was pungent. Dad placed a bowl of grated cheese in the centre. I'd missed Mum's cooking.

Vi and I jabbered at the table. I poured us some squash while Mum took the garlic bread out of the oven.

'Your Bolognese is amazing!' Vi said to my mum, her mouth half-full, tomato sauce dribbling down her chin. 'How are you, Mrs R?'

'Thank you. I'm well, Vi. Truth be told, those first few months I suffered dreadfully with morning sickness, but we're definitely in the blooming phase now!'

As Mum turned around, Vi glimpsed her five-month pregnant bump for the first time. She paled. I knew by her confused expression that when she'd seen Mum weeks ago, she'd just assumed Mum had put on weight.

Now, as Vi puffed her cheeks out, balloon style, wondering what to say, I snorted with laughter.

'What's funny, girls?' Mum was battling with a spatula, so didn't notice Vi's face. 'Seriously, vomit is no laughing matter. I spent so much time in the bathroom with my head hanging over the—well, I'm sure you get the picture.'

Vi elbowed me so hard that my forkful of pasta slopped over the table. 'So . . .' Vi fumbled with her cutlery. 'When are you . . . I mean, when's the thi— baby coming?'

Dad took the plate of garlic bread off Mum as she sat down. 'Halloween!' she said. Then her face fell. 'Didn't Amber tell you the date? We thought it was hilarious.'

Vi bit her lip and stuffed a forkful into her mouth. 'Think I forgot,' she mumbled through spaghetti.

Time to change the subject.

'What exciting things did *you* do?' I babbled, looking pointedly at Vi. 'What have I missed?'

'At school?' Vi said, glancing at my parents.

'I suppose school, but . . .' I shrugged. 'You know, did you do *anything else* exciting?'

'I joined the drama club, but you knew I was going to do that. It's fun. Next term we're doing *Twelfth Night*.' She licked a smear of garlic butter at the corner of her mouth.

'Cool. When are auditions?'

'Soon, I think. Want to help me learn lines?'

'Course!' I tried to keep my voice casual as I

added, 'I was gone for three whole weeks. Nothing else happened?'

'Yeah. No. Not really,' Vi said. 'Oh. Well. I hung out with Taylor a bit. More than I intended.' She gave me a pointed look. 'Layla was off school with tonsillitis. Taylor was alright, but she doesn't get my jokes like you do. *At all.*'

Hearing this made my heart sing.

'Who would, ya weirdo?' I said. Just because Vi had made other friends didn't mean we weren't still close. 'But, you know, maybe if Taylor's not *so* terrible any more then we could all hang out together sometimes?'

'That'd be good.' Vi looked grateful at the effort I was making, considering Taylor had always been my nemesis. But I figured, if I could handle Queen Bea, then I could handle anyone. Nothing like having a gun waved in your face to help you get some perspective.

I realized how much I'd missed all of this. All the normal stuff. Chatting about our day, eating and laughing. There was no . . . danger here.

But just as I let myself relax, the spy phone in my pocket buzzed against my leg.

Here we go again . . .

ABOUT THE AUTHOR

EM NORRY was born
in Cardiff, Wales
and grew up in the
care system, living
in various children's
homes and foster
homes until her early
teens.

In her twenties, Em
lived in London, and
worked in a variety of jobs, from barmaid to video
shop assistant, including her dream job of working
for a year as an editorial assistant.

Em has a BA (Hons) in Film Studies and an MA in
Screenwriting. She also writes short stories and
young fiction as E. L. Norry and Emma Norry.

Em works in admin at Bournemouth University
and writes on her day off and at weekends, often
inspired by her two children.

ACKNOWLEDGEMENTS

It might seem as if a book is written by just one person, because their name is on the front cover, but in reality tens of people are busy behind the scenes all working towards the same goal of making a book the very best it can be for you, the reader.

I'd like to thank my agent, Philippa Milnes-Smith for always being encouraging, enthusiastic, and supportive about my storytelling.

I'd like to thank Liz Cross for believing in me enough to give me this fantastic opportunity.

Next, a big high-five to Gill Sore, ideas whizz and editor extraordinaire, and thanks also to Emily and Emma for their editorial notes, patience, experience, and valuable input. All three are helping make me a stronger, better writer.

I'm grateful to have insightful, thoughtful friends who, as well as being fantastic writers in their own right, were generous with their time and feedback during early stages: Jenni Spangler, Sara Hills, Becca Bell, Wendy Christopher, Susan Conner, Jesse Bryant, and N.T. Franklin.

Thank you, always, to all the readers, libraries, and bloggers—without you, there would be no stories at all.

And to everyone at OUP who have been, and will be, involved in Amber's journey along with me, my deepest thanks and gratitude.

It's been an absolute pleasure.

Em

Ready for more great stories? Try one of these ...